'We have a leak. A bloody big one . . . Right at
the top.'

Mercer could not help the growing unease he
felt which seemed to suggest that he was being
set up. He could sense that the finger of
suspicion was not just pointing at him, but was
prodding him firmly in the chest. His
resignation would have to be held in abeyance
yet again: he could not leave now. That would
look very suspicious. He was trapped.

James Murphy

CEDAR

SPHERE BOOKS LIMITED

SPHERE BOOKS LTD

Penguin Books Ltd, 27 Wrights Lane, London W8 5TZ (Publishing and Editorial)
and Harmondsworth, Middlesex, England (Distribution and Warehouse)
Viking Penguin Inc., 40 West 23rd Street, New York, New York 10010, USA
Penguin Books Australia Ltd, Ringwood, Victoria, Australia
Penguin Books Canada Ltd, 2801 John Street, Markham, Ontario, Canada L3R 1B4
Penguin Books (NZ) Ltd, 182–190 Wairau Road, Auckland 10, New Zealand

First published in Great Britain by Malvern Publishing Company Ltd 1986
Published by Sphere Books Ltd 1987
Reprinted 1987

Printed and bound in Great Britain by
Cox & Wyman Ltd, Reading
Set in Trump

For my mother Laura

'We have been compelled to create a permanent armaments industry of vast proportions. This conjunction of an immense military establishment and a large arms industry is new in the American experience. The total influence – economic, political even spiritual – is felt in every city, every statehouse, every office of the federal government. In the councils of government, we must guard against the acquisition of unwarranted influence ... by the military-industrial complex. The potential for the disastrous rise of misplaced power exists and will persist.'

Extracts from Dwight D. Eisenhower's Farewell Address to the Nation, 17 January 1961.

NOVEMBER 1984
London, England

I

It was after five when Mercer emerged from the gloom of the tube station. A depression over the North Sea had brought a thin drizzle and a scudding wind, and he stopped for a few moments at the top of the steps to button up his overcoat.

He crossed into Parkhurst Road, his shoulders hunched against the rain, his pace even and steady. He kept close to the building line, striding past houses and shops, occasionally swerving around or side-stepping rain-soaked bundles that loomed up before him on the slippery pavement. As he turned into Lansdowne Road, he noticed that the rain had ceased, and he paused to turn down his collar and to glance up at the sky.

Heavy black clouds, like sagging balloons, covered the city and convinced him that it was only a temporary lull. He patted the front of his coat to remove some glistening droplets before continuing on his way. Mercer, like the North Sea, was depressed.

Excited shouts and cries beckoned him from the sports ground on the opposite side of the road and he stopped to see what was happening. Light from the roadside lamps indirectly lit a thin strip of ground which was crowded with dashing figures engaged in soccer practice. The men were shouting and waving, calling for the ball whose whiteness was gradually disappearing under layers of congealing mud. He set off again, certain that he was not being followed.

His route took him past the Gas Works and down to the intersection with Angel Road where he turned left, then right. He stumbled on the uneven pavement, and his feet found a deep puddle which splashed water up around his ankles. He leant against the wall and pulled up his trousers, shaking one foot after the other at the black water. He took one last look round before continuing on his way.

From the main road he wandered off into the back streets that divided row upon row of neat terraced houses. Cars were parked bumper to boot at the kerbsides making the streets little more than alleyways. He headed in the general direction of the Jewish Cemetery before turning off towards another collection of terraces behind Hertford Road.

He reached his destination, a gaily painted pub in the centre of a block of houses, at seven o'clock. He went inside without a second glance.

He ordered a gin and tonic at the bar, then went through to the toilet. He rubbed his matted hair dry as best he could on a paper towel and tried to smooth it flat with his hands. He never carried a comb.

His drink was waiting for him when he returned and he took it over to an empty table. He was on his second gin when Todd came in.

'A guide to the hidden pubs of London. That's what you should write. Move over,' said Todd as he sat down with his whisky.

'Funny,' replied Mercer in a flat voice. He noticed that Todd's raincoat was dry. He kept his eyes on the door.

'I came by taxi if that's what's bothering you. Didn't fancy hoofing around the back streets in this weather.'

Mercer sighed. 'D'you want another?' he asked.

'Do dogs like bones?' said Todd.

At the bar, Mercer could feel Todd's eyes on his back. When he crossed to the juke-box, they followed him. He dropped some coins into the machine and made a long list of selections before collecting the refills. Todd was lighting a cigarette when he came back.

The music filled the room.

2

'This is the last one,' said Mercer, placing the whisky in front of Todd.

'What's up? Broke are you?' said Todd with a grin.

'Meeting, I mean,' said Mercer curtly.

Todd frowned. 'Why? Not because I didn't follow your instructions? I . . .'

'No, no,' interrupted Mercer. He rubbed his eyes. 'It's finished. All over. The Old Man's gone.'

Both men quietly contemplated their drinks.

They were seated in the corner furthest from the door, in an arc of heat thrown out by a glowing coke fire. Close to the fire sat an old man, worn and hunched, nursing a pint of beer that had lost its head. He clung to the somnolent heat which with his meagre pension he could not afford in his own home, his face red and unshaven, eyes almost closed, lost in a world of his own.

At the bar, two young men, suited but tieless, were chatting up the pasty-faced barmaid, telling jokes and stories in between mouthfuls of peanuts which they scooped up greedily from little white bowls at their elbows.

Opposite the door, in the adjacent corner to Todd and Mercer, was the juke-box, flashing alternately red then purple, all plastic and imitation chrome, standing out from the wood and cloth of the bar-room fittings like a Cadillac in a Victorian traffic jam.

'You put this one on?' he asked Mercer.

The two would-be Lotharios suddenly burst out laughing, one of them choking on his half-chewed peanuts, while the barmaid tried to look offended under the layers of powder and cream. The old man snorted himself awake and teased his lips with a lick of beer. *She loves you, yeh, yeh, yeh, yeh*, chanted the Beatles from the speakers set over the fireplace. Mercer tapped out the rhythm with a coaster on the table top. Todd lit another cigarette and smiled broadly.

'Spring of our last year?' Todd nodded agreement. 'I like a bit of nostalgia.'

'Nostalgia's a thing of the past,' said Todd.

'Certainly isn't what it used to be,' replied Mercer routinely. But both men smiled at their old joke.

'So,' said Todd, 'He's gone. Resigned? Sacked? What?'

Mercer bit his lower lip. 'He had a heart attack two days ago.'

Todd waited a few seconds before replying. 'I'm sorry, Joe. Truly I am. I know how close you two were. How bad is it?'

'He's still in intensive care. There's a chance he'll pull through so I'm told. But . . .' He let his voice trail off. He sipped his drink. 'They won't let me in to see him though.' His voice was thick with emotion.

'That's standard practice though, Joe. Immediate family only.'

'I know. I know,' said Mercer. He slipped out of his overcoat. Little pools of rainwater ringed his seat. Todd looked uncomfortable in his raincoat which was buttoned and buckled. 'Can I have a cigarette?'

'Help yourself.' Todd shoved his packet of Gitanes across the table. Mercer took one but refused the offer of a light.

'Still trying to give them up,' he said sheepishly. Todd went for more drinks. He also fed the juke-box again.

'Who's in the hot seat now?' asked Todd.

'His Deputy. Fordyce,' said Mercer.

'And what about you? Surely you must be in with a chance for Deputy?'

'Not a chance. You know that anyway.' Mercer sounded exasperated. 'And even if there was the remotest, outside chance of being offered the position, I wouldn't take it.'

'Why ever not? Keep up the fight. You can't just throw in the towel now. Not after what you and Sir Peter have done.'

Mercer laughed. 'We've done nothing. Merely delayed the inevitable by a few years. They've got all the power now. They hold all the high ground. I'd be powerless even as Deputy. No. I'm leaving. I'm out. We've lost.'

'So the Peterhouse Mafia end up the winners,' said Todd. Mercer picked up their empty glasses. 'Here,' said Todd. 'I'll get them.' He stood up and went to the bar.

When he came back, he was silent for a while. Mercer watched him, and Todd watched the other inhabitants of the bar.

Finally, Todd spoke. 'So. No more cosy chats, eh?' Mercer nodded his head. 'I suppose the Old Man would have gone sooner or later. The heart attack simply made it sooner.'

'There's no need for that, Tom. You can be a bastard at times, you know.'

'Really?' said Todd. 'Look, Joe. The Old Man was lucky to stay this long as Director. He should have gone over the Falklands affair.'

Mercer could feel his face redden. 'It wasn't his fault,' he hissed.

'The Argentinians mount a full-scale invasion of one of our territories and Her Majesty's Secret Service miss it all. Not a squeak. Not a hint.'

'The Americans also claimed to have missed it. Even with all that hardware up in space.'

'But it was British territory. Our responsibility. The Service's responsibility. Sir Peter should have resigned for the Service's failure to spot the Argentinian build-up. The Foreign Secretary did. He took his share of the blame.'

Mercer leant forward across the table. 'It wasn't the Old Man's fault.' He spoke slowly and deliberately as much for Todd's benefit as his own. He was drunk, and his tongue felt thick and heavy. He suspected that Todd had been feeding him doubles. 'The Foreign Secretary was a good friend of the Old Man's. The Prime Minister thought they were both too soft on the Russians. So did the Peterhouse Mafia. They like this present government. Understand?' Todd shook his head and frowned. 'Good God man. Don't you understand what's been happening these past few years? Why we've been meeting like this?'

'Some of it. Most of it probably,' said Todd

'The Old Man stood in the way of the Peterhouse

5

Mafia,' said Mercer as if lecturing to a particularly unintelligent pupil. 'The government was at a low ebb and coming up to a general election. It needed a tonic, a fillip. The Mafia wanted the Old Man out of the way. The Falklands happened to come along at the right time. For both parties.' He spat out the words angrily.

Todd sat back in his chair, a faint smile playing around his lips.

'You're saying that intelligence about the invasion of the Falklands was deliberately and purposefully withheld to put both the Foreign Secretary and the Old Man on the spot. And also to keep the present government in power.'

'You said that. Not me.' Mercer realised that Todd had goaded him along this path with his remarks about the Old Man. But he was not angry with himself. Rather he felt relieved, as if a great weight had been suddenly lifted from his shoulders. He had passed on information to Todd before at the Old Man's behest, but this was the first time he had ever overstepped his brief and leaked unauthorised information.

'All orchestrated by the Peterhouse Mafia,' smiled Todd, pleased with himself. 'With a little help from Cameron in Washington. That was how the Americans claimed to have missed the build up, wasn't it?'

Mercer held up both hands. 'That's enough, Tom. Leave it alone.' He got to his feet unsteadily and walked stiffly to the toilet. He splashed cold water on his face. He felt better. He stared at his reflection in the cracked mirror next to the Durex machine. His hair had dried in the heat from the fire and now stood up in wild clumps, littered with specks of yellow from the paper towel.

'I'm going home,' he announced to Todd when he returned.

'I'll call a cab,' said Todd. He used the 'phone behind the bar. 'Be a few minutes. We'll wait outside.' Todd led the way, followed by Mercer who used one of the tables to offset his stagger.

They stood in the doorway of the pub and arranged to meet again towards the end of January. Todd hinted that there was plenty of work abroad for journalists, particularly those with the sort of contacts Mercer had. Mercer nodded his understanding.

The rain had stopped and the night air, chilly and brisk, had a clean feeling to it. Mercer breathed deeply. When the taxi came, he said he wanted to walk for a while to clear his head. Todd smiled knowingly and allowed himself to be ushered into the car. Mercer waved him off.

Mercer turned left out of the doorway and walked to the corner of the block and turned left again into another street of terraces. Just before the houses began, the dark mouth of an alley was framed between the two lots of brickwork. He ducked quickly into the alley and started to run. The passageway ran the full length of the block in which the pub was situated. He prayed that there wouldn't be any obstacles on the ground to trip him. He passed the back entrance to the pub, swerving to avoid a stack of crates containing empty bottles. He reached the other end breathing heavily, his chest heaving.

He paused for a few seconds to gather himself, then crept forward to the corner. He peered round. Ten yards away, its light spilling onto the pavements, stood the pub. He did not have long to wait.

He heard the scratch of the door as it was pushed open. The pensioner who had nursed his beer all evening swayed out into the street. Mercer pressed himself against the brickwork.

The old man straightened, losing his hunched stance. Further along the street, a set of headlights came to life. The car was eased from its parking space and edged forward slowly towards the man who waved it on impatiently. The erstwhile pensioner climbed into the back seat and the vehicle accelerated away. Mercer pulled himself deeper into the shadows.

As the sound of the car died away, Mercer emerged

from his vantage point and returned to the pub. He used the 'phone to order a taxi for himself, and while he waited, he spoke to the barmaid. No, she had not seen the old gent before tonight. He was not a local, she was sure. 'Just like yourself and your gentleman friend,' she said to Mercer. 'Never seen him in 'ere before.'

On the drive back to his flat, Mercer was worried. The license number of the car was a giveaway: MI5 used those plates for its surveillance vehicles. But what perturbed him most was the fact that his home telephone was being tapped. He had used it to make the date with Todd. And the old man had been in position before Mercer had arrived at the pub.

His vague feelings of the past few days that someone was following him had now crystallized into certainty. What was going on?

II

Todd waited until he was safely and securely locked within his apartment before unbuttoning his mackintosh. A single black wire showed itself sellotaped to the lining. It ran from behind the button hole at the neck down to the right-hand pocket of the coat. Todd carefully pulled the connection free from the hole and shoved the wire into the pocket through the lining after breaking off the sellotape. He took out the tape-recorder from its hiding-place. He rewound the tape, and over a cup of black coffee, he listened again to all that Mercer had said.

Cairo, Egypt

I

Todor Zarev closed the guide-book and stretched full
length on his sun-lounger. A dark cloud swept across
the face of the sun, and the breeze, momentarily de-
prived of heat, brought a chill to the pool area. He
shivered and rolled on his side. It was lunch-time and
the few sun-bathers who had been enjoying the warmth
of the grassy patio now took refuge in the half-enclosed
dining-bar. He decided to eat lunch in his room.

He collected his book and sun-glasses and slipped
into his flip-flops. He slithered towards the side entrance of the hotel. A stand of palm trees, a wind break,
waved gently in the breeze, and above it, the apex of the
Great Pyramid pointed at the clouding sky. The hotel
corridors were dark and cool, reminding him of the
mosques and churches of his native Bulgaria, forbidding
yet inviting, encouraging silence, countenancing only
the barest whisper.

He called down to room service, and while he waited,
he showered and dressed in a white shirt and grey
slacks. He had difficulty in securing the belt around his
large pot belly. He was not very tall, but his bulk gave
the impression of a much bigger man. He had short
arms with huge biceps and he looked like a small, bald
Sumo wrestler.

A waiter in a starched white jacket brought the
club-sandwich and coffee, and Zarev demolished both
in a few minutes. He dozed on the bed for a while until
it was time to go downstairs. Before leaving, he put on a
blue pullover as he knew the air-conditioning in the
lounge would be running.

Downstairs he ordered a whisky and soda and a
packet of Marlboros which the dark-skinned waitress

brought with a smile. He lit a cigarette and dragged deeply, but there was very little kick from the smoke. He longed for one of his own favourite brand, Hercegovina Flor, made from black Russian tobacco. But they were too obvious to have around Cairo. Anyone with a packet would immediately come to the attention of the Secret Police. And that was something he had to avoid.

The waitress brought him another drink without being asked; she knew his routine. While she was at the table he asked for a copy of the local English-language newspaper. He was travelling on a Dutch passport which explained his heavily accented English, and, as he had not noticed a local Dutch one, he had not thought it inappropriate to ask for the English version.

He wondered whether he was being over-cautious, whether he was, perhaps, attributing to the Egyptian Secret Police, powers of observation and detection that they did not possess. He decided he was not.

Anybody visiting Egypt for the first time as he was could not fail to be amazed by the sheer chaos of the place. Cairo in particular. The city was awash with people, and it was nigh impossible to escape from the press of jabbering humanity. Nothing seemed to work, including the people, and his hotel was one of the few islands of sanity in a sea of blaring madness.

He had worked in South America, Africa and the Far East, and his experience warned him that wherever such conditions prevailed, beneath the surface, watching and waiting, would be a highly efficient Secret Police force. The chaos could not exist without some repressive mechanism to forestall the revolutionary forces that would inevitably gather. Egypt would be no exception. After all, he thought, the KGB had had a hand in the training of President Mubarak's forces under his predecessor, Anwar Sadat, and it was a legacy of those turbulent times, the expulsion of the Russian, and the assassination of Sadat, that had brought him to Cairo.

Three men came into the bar just as the waitress

10

delivered his newspaper. He picked it up and began to read, not giving the newcomers a second glance. He already knew their route: he could see it unfold in his mind's eye. The two younger men surveying the faces in the bar; behind them, the tall, stooped figure of Mohamed Aboushanab, his grey head nodding slowly on his thin shoulders, his olive-skinned features showing boredom and indifference as he waited for the necessities to end.

Zarev opened the paper at the centre fold, and looked up. The men were taking their seat at the first table, and a waiter was already on his way over to them with a tray of drinks. Orange juice for the bodyguards, Perrier water for Aboushanab.

They always sat at the same table. Anyone entering or leaving the lounge bar had to pass the table. That was the only chink in their armour. And that was where Aboushanab would die tomorrow.

II

Zarev's contact in Cairo, a scrawny, furtive individual named Ahmed, had delivered a black Samsonite briefcase to Zarev's room the night before. Now it lay on the bed, its contents once again undergoing Zarev's careful scrutiny. He touched each of the items in turn: the small flask of photographer's hypo, the hand-grenade, a British made LIAI anti-personnel device which Zarev had insisted upon as a back-up should his first plan misfire, a metal wrist brace, fitted with a spring and plunger which Ahmed had made to Zarev's specifications, a phial of hydrogen cyanide, one end of which was capped in rubber, the other with a thick needle six inches long, and a further two phials, both empty.

He sat on the end of the bed and took out the brace; he cocked the spring and fitted an empty phial. He tapped the side of the brace against his hip and the spring jumped forward, the plunger depressing the rubber cap down the whole length of the phial. He repeated the process with the other one, and smiled to himself, well satisfied with Ahmed's handiwork.

From under the bed he pulled a square of polystyrene, four inches thick. Using his penknife, he cut it to fit snugly inside the case. Then he hollowed out the centre wide enough to hold the grenade. He emptied the case of those items he would need immediately: the hypo and the phial of poison which he placed on the bedside table. He closed and locked the case and put it in the closet together with the block of polystyrene.

He lay down on the bed and shut his eyes for a few moments. He sat up on one elbow and reached for the hypo. He removed the cork and quickly drank the contents. He held onto the bottle and lay still on the bed for fifteen minutes before groggily getting to his feet. He would have preferred amyl-nitrate to hypo as an antidote to cyanide, but he had to make do with what he could get. He slipped the empty bottle under his pillow and then put on the wrist brace, securing it to his arm with the webbing provided. He put on his jacket. Into the left-hand pocket he placed the phial of cyanide.

It was five minutes to five when Aboushanab's two bodyguards got to their feet and left their employer alone at the table.

Behind his newspaper, Zarev surreptitiously cocked the spring.

A waiter walked over to Aboushanab's table with another Perrier water for the man and a Daiquiri for Madame Lefèvre. Zarev watched through the lacquered trellis-work as the two bodyguards crossed the mezzanine towards the exit.

Three times a week Aboushanab came to the hotel for a sauna and an assignation with one of his many lady friends. Madame Lefèvre was the current favourite. From five o'clock until six-thirty, room 403 would

12

normally witness their couplings. Aboushanab liked to observe the proprieties; he always dismissed his guards five minutes before the lady's arrival.

Zarev finished his drink and began to refold his newspaper. The waiters and waitresses were at the far side of the room chatting and laughing among themselves. A young American couple seated near them made up the lounge population. He quickly inserted the phial into the brace.

He could have killed Aboushanab and his mistress on their way up to their room, or in the room itself. But the KGB's mokrie dela warrant had called for a natural death, even an accidental one. The cyanide would do the trick. He got to his feet and pushed in his chair.

The tables and chairs in the lounge were placed close together and his progress towards the exit was slow and calculated. Aboushanab just sat there at his table, staring off to one side, unaware of his approach. Zarev's arms swung loosely at his sides.

As he neared Aboushanab, he began to time the swing of his right arm to coincide with his arrival at the table. He needed to catch Aboushanab on the upswing so that the needle, lying along his index finger, would be pointing directly in the man's face.

Aboushanab turned to face Zarev at the last moment, as if some instinct had warned him that death was approaching. Zarev smiled as his right arm began the final upswing. He received a faint smile in return.

Zarev's arm struck his hip as it moved forward and up, and he folded his index finger into his palm.

A fine spray, a vapour, mushroomed from the needle and covered Aboushanab's face. He coughed once, then again, his features contorting into a mixture of surprise and fear. He reached for the handkerchief in his top pocket.

Without breaking stride, Zarev dropped his arm casually to his side and continued out of the bar. He passed the souvenir shop and had reached the toilets before the first reaction came. He heard a muffled thud, followed by a crash. Then a pause, broken by a scream. As he made for the elevator, the clamour from the lounge-bar increased. He went straight to his room.

Once inside, he pulled off his jacket and removed the brace. He brought out the briefcase, took out the grenade and laid it gingerly on the bed. Into the case went the hypo bottle, the brace and the empty phials. On top of these he placed the square of polystyrene with the hollow facing towards the lid.

From his suitcase, lying in the folds of a shirt, he took a short length of thin wire. He began to sweat despite the coolness of his room. He sat on the bed, picked up the grenade in his left hand and gripped the plunger firmly, pulling out the pin and replacing it with the wire. Very slowly, he eased his grip on the plunger. The wire held firm against the pressure from the plunger. He let out a sigh of relief.

He placed the device in the hollow of the polystyrene with the plunger pointing upwards, he closed the lid, pushing down hard against the polystyrene. Just as the two halves of the case were about to close on each other, he gently tugged the wire free, secured the clasp and locked the case. He had only just finished when there was a tap on the door. He put the case in the closet before opening the door.

It was Ahmed. He was grinning. Zarev ushered him inside. While he retrieved his case, Ahmed informed him of the sad passing of Mohamed Aboushanab. A heart attack, they were saying. Zarev gave him the case and the key and told him his money was inside together with all the other odds and ends that had to be disposed of. He hurried Ahmed away as fast as he could.

His parting thought as Ahmed disappeared down the fire stairs was the hope that he could contain his greed long enough to wait until he was alone; otherwise the booby-trapped briefcase would claim more than one victim.

London, England

I

Moving from Deputy-Director to Director, one loses an adjective and gains a kingdom, a more forceful handshake, and an air of considered wisdom.

Providing everything is going smoothly. And for Bill Fordyce, as far as Mercer could tell, that was the case. It had even percolated down to the dowdy Mrs Engleton who kept watch on Bill's office. A rise of two floors to the penthouse office suite perched atop Century House had seen the introduction of discreet layers of make-up and a fussy efficiency that in the first week of the takeover had become almost legendary. The shyness and the nervous twitching whenever someone called at her master's office, was replaced by a bold stare and questioning posture. Gone were the apologies for Bill's usual forgetfulness in double-booking appointments without informing her. Now nothing was said, and a show of impatience was met by a baleful glare.

Mercer had been waiting for nearly half an hour for a ten o'clock meeting with his new boss. Mrs Engleton had merely indicated a chair and told him to wait as there was 'someone else with *The Director*.' She used *The Director* both as a reprimand and a warning, much in the same way as a school secretary would use *The Headmaster* to a recalcitrant pupil. Mercer had felt it obligatory to sit and refrain from fidgeting.

The door behind Mrs Engleton opened and the balding head of Leonard Binder peeked out, followed by the rest of his body. He did not look too pleased with himself.

'Thank you, Leonard', said Bill Fordyce as he emerged, and patted him on the shoulder. 'Ah, Joseph,' he added as he spied Mercer. 'Sorry to have kept you

15

waiting.' The pats on Binder's shoulder became a series of pushes as he was propelled towards the door. Mercer stood up.

'Morning,' said Mercer and approached Fordyce who gestured that Mercer should enter. Out of the corner of his eye Mercer saw Mrs Engleton half rise, an angry look on her face. Mercer had obviously transgressed.

Fordyce intervened to prevent a confrontation. 'No more appointments this morning, Anna,' he said sharply, and swung his door shut.

The Director's office had been transformed since Mercer's first visit which was only six days ago. There was not a trace of the Old Man to be seen anywhere. All was new wood, shining chrome and fresh paint. Neatness and tidiness prevailed where once had reigned casual disorder, leaning stacks and fallen piles. Mercer wrinkled his nose at the sweet-sickly fragrance of canned air freshener.

'Sit down, Joseph,' said Fordyce with a smile. Mercer pulled a wooden chair to the front of the desk as Fordyce sat behind it. Mercer waited for the Director to begin, having decided when first learning of the summons, to listen to all that was to be said before speaking himself.

Fordyce settled himself in, sitting forward, his weight on his elbows, his shoulders hunched, his normally long neck telescoped into his chest. He coughed for attention. 'I'll be seeing all my Heads and Departmental Chiefs over the next few days.' He paused and coughed again. 'At a time of, er, change it's always best, I think, to have a little chat with those in charge.' His hands moved to the letter-opener beside the blotter.

'Yes,' said Mercer, keeping his eyes just below the man's chin. He noted the usual pin-striped suit and white shirt with the finely knotted tie which clung to his adam's apple and moved with it as if it had been painted on.

'I don't think any one of us will ever be able to appreciate the great debt that we owe Sir Peter.' Here he raised his eyes to the ceiling as if expecting Sir Peter to be gazing down on them benignly. 'He brought the Service through several, er, sticky patches: Blunt; The Falklands; The Franks Committee.' He picked up the letter-opener and began to prod the blotter. 'But I have no need to remind you, Joseph, about what Sir Peter accomplished.'

There was a hint of bitterness in Fordyce's voice which Mercer quickly detected and understood. Fordyce had only been in the Service five years. He had been brought in after the Blunt revelations as a political appointee with a watching brief from the Cabinet Office. He was a spy sent to spy on the spymaster.

But the Old Man had been too astute. He had simply accepted Fordyce's imposition and then allowed him to get lost amongst the myriad of Departments and Sections that proliferated within Century House. The Peterhouse Mafia found him sympathetic but powerless, while the Old Man's followers simply shunted him around from place to place. As a result he knew very little about how the Service worked or what tasks it set itself. Fordyce, thought Mercer, as the newly-appointed Director of MI6, was the perfect front behind which to operate and scheme.

'The point is, Joseph, that we must continue with the good work. Continue to maintain the standard of excellence. In your case, as Head of Russian Section, that goes without saying.' He sat back in his chair and stroked the blade of the opener across his palm. 'You have always given your best. And I trust you will continue to do so despite the changes that will occur.' He spoke at the desk top, his chin resting on his chest.

'I see,' said Mercer.

'You do? Oh. Good. Thank you, Joseph.' He sat up straight and the expression on his face reminded Mercer of a stupid man who had suddenly found out he had done something clever.

There was a pause. 'Changes?' prompted Mercer.

'Yes,' said Fordyce slowly. 'More a change of emphasis. I am referring in particular to my previous position as Deputy Director.' He chuckled. 'Sometimes, Joseph, I used to feel like the Vice President of America. You know. Fancy title but no clout. The butt of everybody's jokes. Not a nice position to be in really.'

Mercer nodded.

'I envisage a different role for my Deputy!' Fordyce was suddenly very businesslike. 'And the role of Director come to that.'

'I'm sure you do,' replied Mercer.

Fordyce ignored the sarcasm and plunged on. 'I see my Deputy as a man who is involved . . .'

Mercer switched off. All he wanted to hear was the name of the new Deputy. To get it he would have to wade through the Director's grandiose schemes and plans. He was not prepared to do that. His eyes began to glaze over and he was aware of the Director's voice droning on in the background. He recognised his own voice as it periodically entered the fray to record an appropriate response. He was asleep with his eyes open, a trick he had learnt during his days at Oxford in the dull, and very often incomprehensible lectures and tutorials he had attended.

'. . . So, as I said before, the change will be one of emphasis,' concluded Fordyce. Mercer came awake, alerted by the tone of voice. 'What do you think?'

'Yes,' was all that Mercer could muster.

'Good.' Fordyce seemed pleased with himself. 'He's a contemporary of yours. In fact you both entered the Service at the same time.'

Mercer was confused. 'Sorry. Who?'

'Why Alex Cameron of course. Our new Deputy.'

Mercer was mentally composing the phrasing for his letter of resignation as a huge grin broke over the Director's features.

II

Mercer strode through the subterranean corridor that connected Century House with the computer annexe next door. The Old Man had been wrong. He had said that Cameron would never come back after Washington. It's what the Americans call a no-win situation, he had explained to Mercer patiently. 'Remember first of all that one of his predecessors was Kim Philby. And look where he ended up.' The Old Man had chuckled at that. 'If Cameron gets on too well with the cousins, then London won't trust him. London is me, the JIC and the Cabinet Office. That's always been the case. And if he keeps the CIA at arms length to please London, then the CIA will ignore him. He'll have nothing to liaise about. Either way he'll fail.'

The Old Man had sent Cameron to Washington as the Service's liason officer with American intelligence as part of a scheme to break up the entrenched Peterhouse Mafia in London Centre. But Cameron had defied the pundits and was returning to London in triumph, as Deputy-Director of the Service.

He came to the lift shaft. He had to wait. What had Fordyce said just after he had announced Cameron's appointment? 'It's not my decision. That level of appointment is not mine to make, even with the authority I have.' He must have seen the shock registered on Mercer's face, but he had continued blithely. 'Someone's been pulling the strings to get Alex back and I must admit I'm rather pleased to have him working alongside me.' Mercer had a good idea of who had been pulling strings.

The lift came and he got in, pressing the button for the third floor. Fordyce had then stood and walked to the door to indicate that the interview was over. At the door, he had put a hand on Mercer's shoulder. 'He's been doing some tremendous work for us in Washington. With the deployment of *Pershing* in Europe, and our decision to take *Cruise* and *Trident*, it is felt that a much closer and tighter relationship between Britain and America is necessary. Nowhere more so than in the intelligence field.' He had patted Mercer's shoulder twice. 'There's a lot of sense to the appointment, Joseph,' he had concluded. And a lot of double-dealing to boot, thought Mercer.

The security guard on the third floor checked Mercer's credentials and montioned him forward to the ante-room. Mercer picked up the phone, gave his name and asked for Mary Binder. After a few minutes the steel door set in one wall slid open and Mary emerged, wrapped in an anti-static coat cloth. 'Hi, stranger,' she said and kissed him on the cheek. Mercer held on to her arm and guided her to the low settee next to the telephone table. 'What's up?' she asked, concern showing on her face. 'You look awful.'

'I can't make it this weekend,' he said.

'Let me guess. World War Three is about to begin.'

'I need to get away for a few days. On my own.'

'Oh. I've never had that effect on a man before.'

'It's not you,' he said. He squeezed her hand. 'I can't really explain.'

'You don't have to,' she said. She brushed a wayward lock of Mercer's brown hair out of his face. 'I heard earlier this morning. About Cameron.'

'That didn't take long to get about. It hasn't even been formally approved yet.'

'There are no secrets in the Secret Service. Everyone gossips in secrets in this organisation.'

Mercer had to smile. 'What will you do?'

'About the weekend? Probably go down to Leonard's,' she said after a moment's thought. 'He's having a thrash. Someone's paid a bill, I think.' She stood up. 'Are you going to the Lakes?' Mercer said yes.

Washington, America

Zeus lay with Hera and begat Ares, the god of war.

Ares lived in a palace in Thrace with his sister Eris. They loved war for its own sake, taking delight and pleasure in the slaughter of men.

Members of the Ares Club, named after the god, take delight not in the ravages of war, but in the enormous profits to be gained from the prospect of war.

Founded in 1948, the Club restricts membership to the chief executives of those corporations whose names appear on the Pentagon's list of Approved Defence Contractors. For most of its existence the Club has been all-American. That is, until 1980, when the British company, Airwork Industries, chaired by Sir James Ffitch-Heyes, won its first contract with the Pentagon. Sir James had been enrolled immediately, and he made it a special point never to miss the tri-annual get-togethers in the Washington home of the current chairman.

William Don Erikson was elected to the chair in the same year that the present incumbent of the White House was elected to the Presidency. They were good and great friends.

'Our Lobby has been most successful,' said Erikson, addressing the membership. 'The defence procurement budget continues to rise steadily. By the end of next year it will be treble what it was when the President first took office.' He squinted his eyes against the cigar smoke. 'Estimates show that the Pentagon will be spending approximately thirty million dollars per hour, twenty-four hours a day, seven days a week.' He paused for effect. 'And this does not include the finance budgeted for the Strategic Defence Initiative.' Murmurs of approval greeted him. 'Gentlemen,' he continued. 'We are enjoying the greatest peacetime spending spree in history.' Applause.

'Our research and development, our technological expertise, planning and production are far superior to anything the Soviets now possess. The West's Hi-tech embargo of the USSR is hurting her deeply. The Soviets are finding it increasingly difficult to compete with the West. We are leaving them behind – far behind. We are now technically superior in weaponry and destructive capability. With our lead in computer technology, the Soviets can never hope to catch us up.' Erikson surveyed the smiling faces. He sipped some water.

'In short, gentlemen, we have created an imbalance. An unacceptable imbalance. One that is growing in our favour daily. And one that is growing increasingly apparent to even our most myopic supporters, in spite of our efforts on Capitol Hill and in the media.' The smiles faded.

'Of course, we all realise that the present investment in the arms industry, must, one day, die to a trickle. But it must be a day of our own choosing. A time when we have had the opportunity to divest and re-invest. We cannot have the ground cut from beneath us by the peace-niks and our reluctant Allies. We have to think of our stock holders: we cannot leave them with worthless certificates. No, gentlemen, the time for peace will be decided by ourselves.'

The Langdales, England

As he stood at the foot of the tarn for a view over to the Langdale Pikes, tiny scraps of half-remembered information, like flotsam tossed onto the beach by the incoming tide, began to percolate through the fog of his memory. Tarn was a Norse word meaning tear-drop, and while Blea Tarn did not resemble one, Lingmoor Tarn, further up the valley, did. Mercer sat down on a moss-covered rock to rest his weary legs. The rock was damp as was everything else in the early morning mist. He had dressed correctly for the hike: a heavy oilskin kagoule over a thick double-knit sweater, waterproof leggings and a pair of cleat-soled walking boots. But he had forgotten to pack his woollen socks and had had to make do with two pairs of ordinary nylon ones: already he could feel the blisters growing on his feet.

He had fond memories of this corner of England. He had been there as a child with his parents and brother Jim, a gangling youth, ten years his senior, to whom the Lakes was simply a source of rocks and pebbles for skimming across the silent waters. Jim, the first born, had been lost and forgotten by their parents as they had struggled to start a haulage business in Liverpool. And they had succeeded. Mercer had been born in a relaxed period of his parents' life when they were able to sit back and enjoy the fruits of their labour. He had become the apple of their eye. Where Jim had had nothing, Mercer had everything. But there had never been any resentment on Jim's part. He had carried on as he always had, eventually following his father into the family business.

When both their parents had died in a car crash, just after Mercer had completed his finals, he and Jim had been devastated with grief. The deaths had left them rudderless. But at least Jim had the haulage business to divert him. Mercer had had nothing.

He had left university and drifted into teaching. That had been a fiasco. He had lasted barely six months. From there he had drifted into the Service. Drifted? Yes. He was a drifter with one foot nailed to the floor. He could have said no to his tutor from Oxford who had called to see him after he had quit teaching. Could have said no when he suggested he take the Civil Service examination. Could have said no later when the same person organised a meeting with some fellows who were always on the lookout for bright chaps. Could have said no during the introduction, the interview, the probationary period. Could have. But did not. Because he always needed a shove, a prompt. Always had to be led. His mother had pushed him to study. His father had encouraged him to stay on at school. His headmaster had delivered him up to Oxford. And his professor had diverted him into the Service. And never once had he objected or questioned. He went with the tide, drifted with it, and had ended up the way he was today. Still adrift, still looking for a helping hand to lead and direct. The Old Man had gone.

He stood up, wiping the muddy dampness from the backs of his legs, and climbed back onto the path. It was now uneven and undulating and very rough in places, and he continued along it until he reached the road that twisted and turned towards the stone bridge, where he stopped to gather his strength for the return loop of the eight-mile hike. He was out of condition and his whole body was weak and ready to give in. It was silly of him to have even contemplated such a walk in the midst of winter. There had been some snow the week before, remnants of which still decorated the higher peaks, and while the sky appeared clear at the moment, he knew how quickly and how treacherously the weather could close in, bringing with it the risk of exposure.

Despite drifting into the Service, he had readily, and without question, absorbed and assimilated the Service's ethos. He soon came to believe that a secret service, such as MI6, the CIA, or the KGB, reflected the moral climate of the country it served. To him, the KGB was a sinister, murderous organisation, characteristics it shared with the Soviet Union which had spawned it. In contrast, MI6 stood for freedom and democracy, just as Britain herself did.

Even during his training at Fort Monkton, he had never attempted to revaluate this simplistic and idealistic perspective as he studied actual case histories of MI6 operations of the forties and fifties, such as the attempts to destabilise Albania, Hungary and Poland. When he graduated to the active list, he was temporarily assigned to London Centre, and become involved, albeit on the periphery, in the Service's successful coup against Cheddi Jagan in British Guyana. This had been followed by the murderous chaos of plot and counter-plot throughout the African continent. And still he did not question.

He only began to have serious reservations about the Service when it joined up with the CIA to bring down the democratically-elected government of Salvador Allende in Chile. He could not say that he suffered a crisis of conscience then. Yet he felt uneasy, disenchanted with himself. He would not let the problem come to the surface, though it constantly prompted him and demanded resolution. He did his job, did it well, and received his promotions. It was only on his return to London Centre, when he saw and heard of the internecine struggle between the Turks and the Mafia, that he allowed himself the time to re-examine his beliefs. Very quickly, in the light of his experiences, he concluded that the methods and tactics of MI6 were no different from those employed by the KGB. Fine words and fine talk about democracy and freedom did not even enter into it. There was no difference between the KGB and MI6. And if there were no differences between the two agencies, he thought, turning the Service's ethos on its head, what separated the two governments that employed and used them?

He had been on the point of resigning when the Old Man had joined the Service. Mercer had taken to him immediately, and they had become close friends. More than that, really. Mercer became the son the Old Man had never had. The Old Man became the father Mercer had lost.

Under the Old Man's guidance, Mercer came to believe that the KGB was run by men who were no brighter or better than their counterparts in the West; and that the West could still counter the activities of the KGB while maintaining a democratic and moral basis to its handling of security and intelligence. But such an outlook was anathema to the Peterhouse Mafia with their no-holds barred approach to the Russians. And so the battle-lines were drawn.

When he reached the fork in the road, he hesitated. He thought better of continuing along the prescribed route, and instead he walked on to the tiny hamlet of Elterwater which, together with Loughrigg Tarn, guards the eastern approach to Great Langdale. He bypassed the woods, taking the main road that would eventually bring him back to the New Dungeon Ghyll Hotel where he was staying.

Blue-black rain clouds filled the darkening sky by the time he turned off towards his hotel. His mind, as it had been all day, was on other things as he crossed the car park. So he did not notice the blue Rover with the London plates parked in the next slot to his car.

As he came in the main entrance, two men in sheepskin car-coats barred his way. 'Mr Mercer?' asked the shorter of the two. Mercer did not reply. He tried to walk round them, but they moved with him.

'Get out of my way,' said Mercer angrily.

The man who had spoken pulled his identification card from his pocket. He stood directly in front of Mercer and shoved it in his face. Mercer took a step backwards and turned his head to one side. 'Don't be silly, Mr

Mercer,' he said quietly. 'Let's talk about it in the car.'

'I'm on holiday. Do you mind? A few days' leave. All proper and correct. So I don't need you lot around.'

'You've been asked to return to London. For urgent consultation,' said the taller one, stepping closer. 'Come along now. We don't want to disturb the other guests.' He looked from side to side to see if the confrontation had attracted unwanted spectators. But the lobby was empty.

There was no point in arguing any further, thought Mercer. They were under orders to bring him back. And they would make certain he went with them. One way or the other. They were only doing their job. He almost laughed. They were kidnapping him. Some job. 'Give me a minute to pack,' he mumbled.

They followed him upstairs to his room and stood over him while he changed and packed his few belongings into his case. They watched him as he settled his bill and said goodbye to the landlord. In the car park, they asked him for his keys. A third member of the team emerged from the shadows to take them. He would drive Mercer's car back to London. Mercer would have the company of short and tall on the drive back in the Rover.

London, England

Todd stared at Dan Needham's telephone number. 'Which way?' he said to the number. He could not remember the order in which he had transposed the numerals to keep the number secure. Had he switched the first and last of them? The middle two? He could not remember. He threw the book aside in disgust and closed his eyes. He tried to recall the time he had actually written in the number, but it was no use. His mind was a complete blank. 'Damn,' he swore.

He did not think he could find an editor in Britain to handle the story. France, maybe. But it would have less impact over there. He had decided on America. The problem was that he could not go there. He was *persona non grata*. His visa had been revoked in 1981, just after the President had been sworn in. The CIA had taken its revenge. Finally.

Dan Needham was his only trustworthy contact over there. And he had had his share of troubles. Once a syndicated columnist, coast-to-coast, he was now eking out a living on a left-wing periodical with a tiny circulation. The CIA had struck at Dan, too. But Todd was sure that his friend would want to hear Mercer's story, and see it published. The problem now was getting together with Dan.

They had first met at the Sorbonne where Todd had gone for post-graduate studies after coming down from Oxford. They had both been involved in the students' revolt in the mid-sixties, when protest and demonstration was the order of the day. Both had also witnessed, in the background, the hand of the CIA. From Paris they went to Vietnam to report the war, and once more the CIA had raised its ugly head. Then Needham had returned to America, his reputation established, while Todd had roamed the world as a freelance. They had joined forces again over Watergate and its aftermath, and had seen the CIA emasculated under Carter.

He had also kept in touch with Mercer down through

the years on his frequent visits to London. They had even met up once in Moscow during Mercer's tour of duty there. Their friendship was deep and genuine and had not been blighted by the different directions their lives had taken since their time at Oxford.

Todd had been in America at the time of the Iranian crisis. He had seen a wave of radical militancy develop throughout America which had displaced the liberal inertia of the Carter days, and had resurrected the war cry of God, Guts and Guns. And it was about that time that Mercer had come to him with information about Sir Anthony Blunt. Dan Needham had used the story in America with Todd's assistance, and both men thought they were on to another Watergate. But Carter's defeat in the Presidential elections had put an end to all that.

With a little plastic surgery, the CIA was rehabilitated, and Todd found himself banned from American shores. Needham was boxed in too. Since that time, the two men had only contacted each other on a couple of occasions by telephone. They were both wary of possible CIA intrusion, so they continued their work independently of each other – Todd in London, Needham in Washington. Times would change, Todd kept telling himself. And Mercer's information, a little here, a little there, indicated that that would soon be the case.

Now Todd felt he had a story, well documented enough to publish. A story which could, perhaps, lift the mood of right-wing rhetoric that had spread from America to infect Britain. But he had to contact Needham. Let him listen to the tapes. What was his bloody number? he thought.

St Albans, England

'I take a very dim view of such behaviour, particularly from a man with twenty years' service,' huffed Sir Humphrey Middleton.

Mercer was no longer angry. The anger had abated on the long drive down from Cumbria. 'And the nature of the urgent consultation that necessitated the Gestapo tactics?' asked Mercer. He was no friend of Middleton's. They had crossed swords on more than one occasion. As the newly-appointed Deputy Under-Secretary of State at the Foreign Office, Middleton chaired the Joint Intelligence Committee, the pinnacle of the intelligence set-up in Britain. He was a government appointee, a member of the Peterhouse Mafia, who had been rewarded for his sterling anti-Russian attitude by his promotion to the chair. Mercer had met him on several committees and boards, and had never liked the man.

Middleton pulled the cord of his silk dressing gown tighter as if it were a garotte conveniently looped around Mercer's neck. 'I will not have impertinence in my home. Not at this hour of the night,' he thundered.

'Day,' corrected Mercer. 'It's after two in the morning and I've been up since six yesterday. I'm tired.' He yawned widely, making no attempt to hide it.

Middleton marched over to the fireplace. He stabbed at the dying embers with a long brass poker, but all he got was a wisp of smoke and a microscopic glow which quickly surrended to the accumulated ash. Middleton's ears threw out more heat than the fire.

Fordyce put a hand on Mercer's shoulder and directed him towards a chair. 'Sit down, Joseph. We're all tired. It's been a long day for all of us.'

Middleton had his hands behind his back as he turned to face Mercer again, his body framed by the wooden mantlepiece. 'An officer of your rank and seniority cannot simply resign, then take off for some god forsaken hidey-hole as if he were leaving a job on a building site.'

'The English Tourist Board would be very interested in your description of the Lake District, I'm sure.' said Mercer. He closed his eyes.

'An explanation is required,' shouted Middleton. 'And I demand one this minute.'

'That's the least we would have expected of you, Joseph,' said Fordyce.

'I had some leave due. I simply thought that this was a good time to take it,' said Mercer.

'Your resignation,' said Middleton, barely able to control his rage. 'What do you mean by it?'

'That's very simple. I'm resigning. Leaving. Getting out.'

'A new Director for the Service. An imminent change of leadership in Moscow,' shouted Middleton 'And you decide to resign and indulge in a spot of fell-walking. You must be mad. These are difficult times for the Service.'

'I thought my resignation might please you,' said Mercer with a smile.

'All in all the timing hasn't been very good, has it, Joseph?' Fordyce was looking at Middleton as he spoke.

A Filipino woman appeared in the room carrying a silver tray on which there were two cups, a pot of tea, and a plate of biscuits. She placed her burden on the small circular table at Mercer's elbow. 'Thank you, Imelda.' The woman bowed and hurried from the room. 'My advice to you, sir,' warned Middleton 'Is to listen very carefully to everything Mr Fordyce has to say to you.' He came and stood over Mercer and wagged a finger in his face. 'Otherwise, things could become very difficult for you.' With that he strode out of the room.

Fordyce poured the tea. There was no sugar. Mercer nibbled a biscuit while Fordyce remained standing, holding his saucer in one hand and cup in the other. 'Is your resignation to stand, Joseph?'

Mercer was beginning to get irritated at the use of

Joseph and the paternal hand on the shoulder. 'After today's episode? – what do you think?' he said sharply.

'You won't reconsider?'

'No.'

Fordyce began to pace. 'Humphrey is quite correct in what he says. The Service is going through a difficult period.'

'That wasn't how you put it the other day. Then it was all talk of a smooth transition and a change of emphasis,' said Mercer sarcastically.

'True,' said Fordyce without a pause. 'But then I was simply talking about the internal mechanics of the Service. I had assumed, mistakenly perhaps, that you were aware of the external problems facing us, and of my relative, er . . .'

'Inexperience?' said Mercer.

Fordyce gave him a cold stare. 'Have it your own way, then.' He came closer to Mercer. 'Suffice it to say that we are facing both internal changes and external problems.'

'And you need me to help out.'

'Good grief, man. What's come over you? The Service has been your life. Are you just going to abandon it without a second thought?'

'I've given it a lot of thought. I want out. I've had enough.'

'This is ridiculous.' Fordyce put his cup and saucer down on the table. 'Joseph,' he said. He put out a hand towards Mercer who shrank back in his seat and raised his cup to his lips. Fordyce straightened up.

'I'm leaving,' said Mercer.

'Perhaps I should have managed our little talk differently? Given you an explanation as to why you were not promoted to Deputy? Broken the news of Cameron's appointment a little better?' continued Fordyce.

'I wouldn't have taken the Deputy's position even if it had been offered,' replied Mercer sourly.

'Sir Peter's illness, then? The latest report is extremely optimistic.'

'Can I go now?'

Fordyce let out his breath in a long, meaningful sigh. He shook his head from side to side and clamped his lips together. Finally he spoke. 'Cameron is not due back until mid-December. He'll need a few weeks in which to settle in. Then there's your yearly assessment for the JIC for February.'

'What do you want exactly?' asked Mercer.

'Your co-operation and your help.'

'And if I refuse?'

'You heard what Humphrey said. Things could become very difficult for you.'

As if they weren't already, thought Mercer. 'You'll have to spell that out for me,' he said wearily.

'Well, you could leave the Service and never find gainful employment again. Overseas travel would never be an option for you. I think you know the story.'

'I thought that sort of thing only went on in Russia,' said Mercer, recalling his thoughts of the afternoon.

'My dear chap. In Russia they would simply shoot you.' Fordyce laughed quietly to himself.

'Tell me, then. Before I fall asleep.'

'Hold your resignation in abeyance for a couple of months. Until March, April, say. Cameron should have worked himself into the job by then.' He sat down and crossed his legs. 'Then there's your assessment for the JIC.'

Mercer thought Fordyce was growing more pompous by the minute and he was happy to be leaving. He would be shot of them all. He agreed to Fordyce's proposals — and was driven back to his flat by the two Special Branch officers. His car was parked outside.

DECEMBER 1984
Tmassah, Libya

I

His knees gave way. As he fell forward he managed to bring his right arm across his face to protect it from the sand. He could feel the coarse grains digging into the exposed flesh and clinging to the damp clumps of hair. His mouth was wide open and his nose pressed against the back of his hand. He swallowed the hot, searing air as a thirsty man gulps down water.

The sand began to move away from his head. 'Tired?' said a voice from above. Tawfiq did not reply; he did not have the strength to. 'You mother-fucker,' snarled the voice. Tawfiq slowly raised his head. The sweat from his brow temporarily blinded him and he had difficulty in focusing. But he knew who it was. He saw a boot which swung away, out of his line of vision, and then he felt its impact as it crashed down into his back. His body shook, but not from pain, as his back had been numbed for an hour or more from the weight of the heavy pack he carried. It was hate that caused his body to snake. 'You Palestinian nigger, you. Get your ass over that fucking hill. Now.' There was a note of hysteria in the voice and Tawfiq knew that Wilson would be armed. Another kick. Tawfiq pushed himself to his knees, then to his feet.

Twenty yards away stood Wilson's truck. In the driver's seat sat his grinning factotum, Ali Ahmed. He waved cheerfully to Tawfiq. He had not heard the truck drive up.

'Move,' shouted Wilson and swung another kick at Tawfiq. 'Get your fucking ass into gear.' Tawfiq set off again. He could see the top of the hill. It did not seem too far away, but already his legs were screaming for another pause. He rubbed his face in both hands not caring about the sand that tore at his flesh. He had to get to the top, to show those bastards.

He staggered forward, digging his heavy boots into the yielding slope. On and upwards. The sky was clear, white almost, like the heat that blasted down from the sun. He had not expected it to be this hot. The night had been cold and he had dressed to combat it. He had no idea that Wilson would try to keep him going all day, too, and would not even give him time to strip off some of the layers. He thought he heard the truck move off. He stopped and was about to turn around when a single shot rang out. A fountain of hot sand exploded at his feet. He continued the climb.

Ali Ahmed's grinning face appeared before him: he struck out at it but it vanished in the still air. He pressed on, the pain in his legs and chest a constant spur, his hatred of Wilson and the revenge he would seek, a distant hope that drew him forward.

He reached the summit without knowing it, blinded by sweat and anger: his legs, on meeting the level ground could not cope with their release from the uphill struggle, and they buckled beneath him. He reeled and staggered before pitching forward, and he tumbled head first down the slope. He had no control, no strength to organise his limbs to afford himself protection as his falling body became wrapped in the broiling sand and was battered and scored by boulders and rocks.

The sand got everywhere: in his eyes, his nostrils, his ears. He could now feel pain in his back, as if it had been rubbed fiercely with an abrasive. He began to cough, then splutter. He tried to sit up but could not and he rolled over onto one side instead. He saw the boot again.

'Beat ya,' laughed Wilson. He placed his boot on Tawfiq's temple and began to push Tawfiq's head deeper into the sand. 'Tomorrow you do it all over again. Without any breaks. If you want a break, ask me. Leg. Arm. Neck. Don't be shy to ask.' He pushed harder until Tawfiq's head was partially buried. 'See you at chow time,' he said, his voice friendly. 'Bye for now.'

Tawfiq was breathing through his nose as his mouth was full of sand. Slowly he extricated himself and shook his head. He could not open his right eye as it was full of gritty particles. He undid the pack strap and shook himself free of its weight. He got to his feet, and then dropped to his knees. He could not find his water bottle. And Wilson had gone. He had no water. He groped blindly, searching for the bottle, but he could not find it. The bastard wants me to die of thirst, he swore to himself. He stopped looking and sat down, a wave of self-pity overcoming him. The bastards, he swore. The desert heat would kill him in a few hours.

He needed shelter from the sun to stop the dehydration. He stood and looked around. He almost fell over in surprise. The camp gates were less than a hundred yards away on his left. He had been running around in circles for hours.

II

Tawfiq woke with a start. It was morning. He climbed out of his bed, his whole body still stiff and sore from the previous day's exertion. He walked over to the window. The sun was well up but not as bright or as strong as yesterday. Clouds flitted across the sky and a strong wind was blowing, rattling the corrugated iron of the roofs. He dressed in dungarees and slipped into his boots before making his way to the mess hall. What was Wilson up to? he asked himself. Why hadn't he come for him as he had promised?

He entered the hall and saw Wilson at one of the tables surrounded by a group of trainees. Tawfiq approached slowly, unsure of himself, and sat down. Wilson was giving a demonstration. On an oily cloth before him lay the stripped parts of a hand gun. 'It's small,' Wilson was saying. 'People call it a woman's gun because it will fit into a small bag. But it's got plenty of stopping power.' Tawfiq recognised the weapon as a 9mm Hertal Bayard. Wilson began to reassemble it. 'Morning, Tawfiq,' he said without looking up and Tawfiq nodded to the group.

'Okay,' said Wilson wrapping the automatic in the cloth. 'Let's get some coffee.' The men began to move off towards the coffee machine. Wilson motioned Tawfiq to stay. 'How d'you feel this morning?' He smiled at Tawfiq. 'Not too stiff, I hope?' His voice sounded sincere.

Tawfiq could not cope with Wilson's changes in temperament, from the savage brutality of yesterday in the desert, to the friendly concern of today. He did not understand the man, and he found it difficult to direct and control his hatred when he met him in this kind of mood. 'I'm okay,' he replied.

'Ali Ahmed's waiting for you in the truck. He'll take you across to Marzuq.' Tawfiq eyed him suspiciously. 'Don't look at me like that,' he said. 'Nothing to do with me. Orders. There'll be a plane at Marzuq to take you to Bel Al Azizir.' Wilson stood up. 'Get packed. Leave as soon as you're ready.' He held his hand out to Tawfiq.

Tawfiq got to his feet. He looked at the proffered hand. He suddenly grasped it and slapped it a couple of times. It was a mechanical gesture; he wished it was Wilson's neck. He pulled free and without a word turned and left. He knew what Wilson's intention was and he did not want to hear the usual crap of the passing-out speech, all that nonsense about being hard on the trainees so as to make them tough, and nothing personal in anything said and done. Crap.

It was all crap, Tawfiq told himself, as he threw his few belongings into a haversack. He hated Americans,

37

Wilson especially. And the other CIA renegades. They might be helping Gaddafi and the Palestinian cause, but they were mercenaries. Big-mouthed Americans who thought that because they knew it all they could treat everybody like shit.

Tawfiq was furious. Why was he being sent to Bel Al Azizir? What could they want with him in Gaddafi's stronghold? He wanted to stay at Tmassah to even the score with Wilson.

Ali Ahmed was waiting for him near the main gate. Tawfiq greeted him coolly and they drove off in silence into the desert towards Marzuq.

He did not like the desert. As a boy in the Gaza Strip he had grown up with it all around him, a stony wasteland that stretched as far as the eye could see on either side of the Jabalyah-Gaza highway.

He hated the nights in the desert, in particular when the temperature dropped and the silence fell, sharp and fragile, like a crystal cocoon, enveloping and hushing the sounds of life.

The nights always reminded him of Israeli soldiers. They had come to their farm at Jabalyah in the dark. Dusty and dirty, insolent and cruel. They had driven Tawfiq and his parents across the desert, guided by the flashing beacon of the troop-carrier to the oasis at Beit Lahiyah. There they were ushered into a huddled family reunion around the shattered body of Ibrahim, Tawfiq's brother, his parents' joy.

He had never seen violence close up before. But he was not ill. What seemed like a steel hand had gripped his stomach and held him together. He had looked with detachment at the bloodied body of his brother and had then backed away to leave his parents to their mourning.

Later the Israelis came again and bulldozed their home. They moved to the West Bank. By the time he was eighteen, Tawfiq had already been held on three occasions at the notorious interrogation camp at Al

Farrah. At twenty, he was in Syria undergoing training as a revolutionary soldier, training that he had thought was tough until he came to Libya.

'Marzuq,' said Ali Ahmed, interrupting his thoughts. Tawfiq could see nothing but the scrub of the desert all around. 'Over the next ridge,' said Ali Ahmed.

III

On the third day after his arrival at Bel Al Azizir, Tawfiq was rudely awakened before dawn by a kick from a woman dressed in green combat dungarees. He started to protest but was silenced by a prod in the ribs from the muzzle of a Kalashnikov. She told him to dress and follow her.

He did as he was told. Gaddafi's personal guards, the Green Nuns of the Revolution, were not to be argued with. She took him to the north side of the camp. 'Over there,' she pointed. 'The building. You are expected.' She left him.

Mohamed Qaja was waiting for him inside. Tawfiq recognised him from the photograph that hung below that of the Libyan leader in the mess hall. Qaja was head of Libyan Intelligence, and as such was responsible for the assassination squads that roamed the Western world seeking out the enemies of the State. He wanted Tawfiq to work for him. In Malta.

The following day, Qaja and Tawfiq flew into Luqa airport. Passport formalities were short because of the close ties between the two countries. A car was waiting for them when they emerged from the arrivals hall. Neither man paid any attention to the scruffy individual at the barrier who carried a board on which was written, in Arabic and English, the names of three men. Nor did they notice the battered Volkswagen that followed them into Valetta and up to the offices of Eastern Translation Services directly opposite the Libyan People's Bureau in Sliema.

London, England

I

'The last time they met the target was in 1980. Three-hundred and sixty tonnes from a grand total of 613 million tonnes produced.'

'Where is it on the map, Tom? I can never remember.'

'That made Russia the world's leading oil producer for that year,' added Tom Irwin as he went around behind Mercer's desk to the large scale map of the USSR. 'There. In the West Siberian Plain. Approximately midway between Omsk and Sverdlovsk.' He pointed at a tiny circle, criss-crossed with red and black lines.

Mercer joined him and pulled his spectacles down from his forehead onto his nose. 'Sverdlovsk?' he said slowly.

'Formerly Ekaterinburg,' said Irwin. He looked across at his superior and saw the questioning expression. 'Where the Tsar and his family were allegedly murdered at the Ipatiev House in 1918.'

'Ah, yes. I thought it sounded familiar for some reason.' Mercer inclined his head. 'Tara River,' he read.

'Tyumen is one of the oldest Siberian towns. It's on the Trans-Siberian Railway.' He pointed again. 'The red line. And it's a river port on the Tara.' He half-turned to face Mercer. 'Tyumen overtook Baku as the leading Russian oil-producing centre back in the sixties. It has vast reserves.'

'Okay, Tom,' said Mercer sitting down. He was not in the mood, nor did he have the time, for one of Irwin's interminable lectures. He began to read the report quickly. Irwin hovered on the periphery of his vision.

He read how inhospitable Tyumen was: mosquito infested during the summer, deathly cold and snow-covered during the autumn, winter and spring. Despite the high financial inducements, experienced oil-field personnel from Baku would not stay there. Training of the next generation of workers was non-existent. More and more, less experienced men took control of the Industry.

To meet their quotas, management concentrated on exploiting known reserves. To do this, exploration programmes were either cancelled or drastically curtailed so that the exploration rigs could be brought in to drill production wells. At first, this worked. Quotas were met. But reserves were being severely depleted as reservoir pressures were reduced. To offset that, non-producing wells were drilled, into which water was injected in order to maintain the reservoir pressure. More drilling rigs were therefore needed. All exploration ceased as management looked only at the short-term quest to keep up production.

But then the fields ran dry. Rigs stood idle without exploration programmes to keep them busy. Production plummeted. 'Serious,' said Mercer, looking up.

'Very,' said Irwin. 'They met production in '82 and '83. Just. A few heads rolled. As far as we can ascertain, '84 has been a total disaster. There's been a massacre up at Tyumen.'

'Where does that leave the Russian oil industry?'

'Well, it'll be at least five years before any new exploration programme bears fruit,' said Irwin.

'Why so long?'

'Well, it's never been a very efficient industry. A lot of equipment, and some of the technology is out-dated. The Russians haven't kept up with new developments and techniques. Of which most come from the West: North Sea and Alaska.'

'I get it,' interrupted Mercer. 'The West's Hi-tech embargo.'

'Exactly. Unless there's a miracle out in Tyumen, Russia will become a net importer of oil in the not too distant future. And she doesn't have the foreign reserves for that. Not with another bad harvest to come. The summer wasn't kind to her again.'

II

The lights in Mercer's office were blazing. The busy clack from the other rooms on the sixth floor had long ceased. He checked his watch. 'Eight-twenty,' he told himself. It was later than he had expected and he was barely halfway through the mountain of paperwork that was perched accusingly on the desk. He arched his back and felt the relief flood through his shoulders, then he rubbed his tired eyes. He had put down his reading glasses somewhere during his discussion with Tom Irwin and he had not been able to find them since. His eyes would be red raw in the morning after working for so long in artificial light.

He picked up Page's report again and flicked through it to the index. He found the Inspection Commission's document. It was a poor photostat, barely decipherable, but Page had gone over the Russian characters in black ink in the more important sections, so that they stood out from the rest. He read about the tractor factories in Siversky and Tobolsk that existed only on paper; about how the management teams had collected salaries for over 800 phantom employees and had falsified production quotas and delivery schedules, all with the connivance of the local Party bosses and representatives of the farming collectives. Even the Ministry of Agricultural Machinery in Moscow had been implicated in the scam. Meanwhile, many farmers were still awaiting the delivery of their duly authorised tractors, and thousands of tractors stood idle, lacking replacement parts that Siversky and Tobolsk were meant to supply. Crops were not planted on time; and those that were, rotted in the fields as the farmers, lacking mechanical assistance, were unable to harvest them before the rains came.

When this kind of activity was combined with the vagaries of Mother Nature, it was easy to understand the annual crop disasters that plagued Russia.

Mercer shook his head at the scale of the fraud. He turned over the pages. They were filled, he saw, with other examples of swindles, *pripiska*, as the Russians called them. Billions of roubles were involved. It was not a new phenomenon: it had been going on since the Revolution, and no doubt would continue for many years to come. It was endemic in the Soviet system. What impressed Mercer was the sheer size of the theft and the audacity of the perpetrators: the stakes were huge, and seemed to grow year by year, as did the number of people involved. The impression Mercer obtained was of a bureaucracy that had thrown in the towel and had given itself over to the illegal exploitation of its own lethargic, incompetent self. It didn't need a genius, or Page's rather pedantic summary, to conclude that without the *pripiska*, Russia could have had a relatively successful Agricultural Industry. The planning, the expertise, the enterprise, that went into the frauds, if put to legitimate use, would have been of untold value to the State.

Earlier in the year, Mercer had received a report from one of his agents detailing the execution of Deputy Minister of Fisheries, Alexei Ritov. He had masterminded a ring that smuggled Beluga caviar to the West in tins labelled herring. The scandal had only come to light when one of Ritov's couriers had bribed a port official with a crate of the tins, rather than the money he was supposed to have used. The official's wife, fearing that her husband would be drawn deeper into the fraud, persuaded him to take the matter to his superiors. They in turn contacted the Criminal Police of the Public Prosecutor's Office, and Ritov had been unmasked.

The case of the Deputy Minister, Ritov, clearly showed that the thieving was not just confined to the middle-ranking apparatchiks, but went all the way through the System to the very top. Even Brezhnev's son-in-law had been implicated in various black market enterprises, as had other members of the General-Secretary's clique, despite the immense privileges they already enjoyed as nomenclatura. It seemed to Mercer that the ship of state was sinking and the rats were preparing to abandon it; but not before they had emptied it. A list of Russians holding numbered Swiss accounts would make very interesting reading, he thought.

He stood up. If the *pripiska* continued unabated, continued to grow, involved more and more of the top people, then the West would never have to fire a rocket at Russia in anger. Russia would bring itself down, the rot spreading eventually from the inside so that collapse was inevitable. He leafed through Page's paper again. There it was – Russia imported a third of the excess grain produced by the Western Democracies – and that was in the years when the harvest had been relatively good. After a disastrous one the figure was more than half and paid for by dwindling reserves of oil, and gold, at a time when gold prices were falling. It was a good job the oil price was holding up. He slipped into his jacket. Irwin had promised all the reports by the end of next week. Hopefully, he could tie everything together the week after that in preparation for the JIC, providing Fordyce and Cameron did not interfere. He had one more look round for his spectacles, but could not see them. 'They'll turn up,' he said. And he began to turn out the lights. It would pay the West, he suddenly concluded as he locked the door, to ensure that Russia never ever had a good harvest. Without the sale of the excess grain to Russia, the West could be in dire financial straits.

Dublin, Ireland

Todd pressed the eject button and the tape jumped out of the player set in the dashboard. The sound quality was not very good and the drone of aircraft overhead had not helped. But Needham seemed to have taken it all in.

'Hmm,' said Needham. He sounded like a buzz-saw. 'Interesting.'

Todd put the tape in his pocket. He was disappointed with the response. 'Look. Let me fill you in on the details. They're all on the other side of the tape but it'll be better if I tell it.'

Needham looked at his watch. 'Flight's in an hour.'

'Okay,' said Todd. 'Right back to the beginning.' He stretched his legs and half turned towards Needham. 'Back in the fifties the Service was being run by the old war warriors who were still patting themselves on the back for Hitler's defeat. They had little or no idea about the Soviet threat. When Burgess and Maclean defected there was a shake up and a few resignations and retirements. A new intake of young officers arrived. It wasn't long before these bright young men came to the conclusion that there hadn't been a wide enough clear out, and they believed the Service was totally compromised.'

Needham passed over a cigarette and opened a window. Todd drew deeply a couple of times before continuing. 'This group was christened the Young Turks. And they turned the Service upside down in their search for moles. Philby's defection in 1963 only strengthened their case and renewed their challenge to the old leadership. As a result, the Service was crippled, paralysed.'

'That's all been well documented,' said Needham with a touch of impatience.

'Right,' said Todd. 'But while all this was going down, new faces were appearing in the Service as the old-timers fell away. A man called Markfield was put in charge of Internal Security, assisted by a colleague who has just been made Deputy-Director of the Service. Okay?' Needham nodded. 'Markfield introduced positive vetting to the Service, not only for new recruits but also for serving officers. Markfield and his assistant graduated from Peterhouse College, Cambridge. Naturally many of the recruits who passed through the vetting were former Peterhouse men. And all of the serving officers whose vetting was not one hundred percent positive were not former Peterhouse graduates.'

'How come?' asked Needham.

'Do you remember Golianov? The KGB Colonel? The one who defected in Copenhagen to the CIA in '61.

'The guy Angleton took under his wing?'

'Yes. Angleton headed the CIA's counter-espionage group at the time. Golianov became his pigeon.'

'He convinced Angleton that the West was being subverted by a world-wide campaign of Soviet disinformation.'

'That's right,' said Todd, taking up the narrative again. 'Nothing was as it seemed. All was apparently illusion, conjured up by the KGB. Disinformation became the key word. And Golianov pointed to the iconoclastic Young Turks as a prime example of the campaign's success. They were tearing the Service apart in the belief, fostered on them by Soviet disinformation, that the Service was rife with moles. Meanwhile the Service's main task of countering Russian influence and infiltration was being ignored.' Todd paused as a Garda patrol car cruised through the car park. He watched it join two others parked next to the taxi rank.

'Markfield was in the same camp as Angleton and Golianov,' said Needham.

Todd nodded. 'And of course this put him at odds with the Young Turks.'

'So he began to weed them out with his positive vetting.'

'Precisely. And so the rise of the Peterhouse Mafia began. They began to give the Young Turks a taste of their own medicine.' Todd rubbed his hands together. 'And now we come to the real dirty end of the business. Markfield uncovered Blunt's treachery, but suppressed it. He couldn't have that out in the open during the fight for supremacy over the Turks. The Peterhouse mob believed in an all out, no-holds barred approach to the Soviets. The Young Turks took a more moderate stance. They had to be removed. News of Blunt's treason would have given them invaluable ammunition.'

Needham checked his watch again. 'So where does your informant, the guy on the tape, fit in to all this?'

'He joined the Service at the time of the Philby defection. He managed to keep apart from the internal squabbling, did his job well, and progressed. Then he came under the patronage of Sir Peter Ralston who was appointed Director of the Service in the late seventies to sort out the in-fighting. Now Ralston believed that the Young Turks were correct but somewhat over-zealous in their hunt for moles. He had no time for Markfield and his merry men. So Ralston leaked the news of Blunt's treachery in the hope of shutting down the Peterhouse Mafia.'

'Didn't the Prime Minister spill the beans on Blunt?'

'Yes. In the House of Commons. But only because it was due to be documented in a book that was about to hit the bookstalls.'

'That's right. I remember now.'

'But Ralston had underestimated the power of the Peterhouse Mafia. They had well-placed friends and allies in Westminster and Whitehall. They just wouldn't lie down. So Ralston made known certain well-founded suspicions that one of the Directors of MI5 had been in fact, a KGB mole.'

'Roger Hollis?'

'Yes. And again it came up in the House of Commons. But this time, the Prime Minister sided with the Peterhouse Mafia. They had been ready for this. We were told that the case against Hollis was just another example of Soviet disinformation. This was a severe set back for Ralston.'

'Quickly followed by the Falklands,' said Needham.

'And then the Franks Committee, which was set up to look into the apparent failures of the Service. The re-organisation of the top secret Joint Intelligence Organisation and the Joint Intelligence Committee meant that the Peterhouse Mafia were able to put their people in all the right places. My informant, if he was to stay in the Service, would have been helpless. Totally under the control of the Mafia. He was very close to Ralston. Almost like a father and son relationship. Always referred to him as the Old Man. Of course he blames the Mafia for Ralston's illness.'

'What's his motive then? Revenge?'

Todd shrugged his shoulders. 'Perhaps that's part of it. I don't really know. He's a strange guy. I've known him for years and I still can't fathom him. He's afraid though. I can see that.'

'He has a right to be,' said Needham. 'Seems to me that you now have a Service much the same as our CIA. Pathologically anti-Soviet and doing more than its share of formulating government opinion. The tail wagging the dog.'

'You could be right.'

'Has your man documented any of this for you? Anything down in black and white that I could show to my editor?'

'No. Is it really necessary? We didn't have it when we went after the CIA during Watergate.'

'The climate was right then – but times have changed. My editor would want to see something. It's a pity you didn't push him harder when he was down over Ralston's illness. He might have come up with something.'

'Perhaps,' said Todd. 'Anyway, I spoke to him last week. He's not leaving until April. And he was as mad as hell about something. I think that when he does eventually leave, it's going to be difficult to stop him talking.'

Fuengirola, Spain

I

It was that dream again; the jungle, the trail, hot and humid. His sweat enveloped him like a confining bag of cling-film. He was running, wild-eyed and terrified, along the beaten track, his arms windmilling in front of him, pushing away the foliage; the tendrils, green and luscious, grabbed at him and his sodden clothing, trying to ensnare him, to slow him down.

His breathing was hard and rasping and his eyes bulged with the effort of sustained exertion and blind panic. His footsteps rapped out a rhythm on the twisting track and the thunder of blood in his ears deafened him to the scraping and screaming of the disturbed jungle.

But then, above it all, came the steady, unrelenting beat of naked feet slapping the beaten earth. One, two. One, two. The sound of pursuit drove him on, yet wore him down, sapping his strength, as he increased his pace to escape.

Then up ahead – the clearing – a sanctuary of brightness that beckoned him from the murk of the matted jungle. The rays of the sun slashed down in steamy beams, a haven into which he stumbled. His saliva was stringy and he could not clear his mouth as he gasped for breath, coughing and choking. He leant against a tree trunk and brushed the moisture from his brow. Then he pushed on across the clearing but was halted by a sudden burst of silence.

He stopped and stared and rubbed his eyes. There, on the edge of the clearing, stood his pursuer. Jackson groaned and his knees sagged. He had been running towards the man, not away from it. He moaned loudly as he recognised the slight figure, bronzed and muscular, that barred his path.

The Mountegard tribesman was naked except for a red loin-cloth pulled high up onto the waist. His black eyes forced Jackson down to his knees in a gesture of supplication. Jackson looked up at him as he nimbly took two steps forward and neatly severed Jackson's head from his body with one deadly sweep of his curved sword.

II

The dream was always the same, though less frequent now. He no longer woke screaming in a pool of chilling sweat, the topsy-turvy jungle and its shrill noises were the last things his dreaming senses registered as his bloody head bounced along the hardened track. It was getting better. The doctors said it would go away one day.

Yet he wondered whether it would go, just to be replaced by another, equally as disturbing, constant reminder of his days in Vietnam. It was this that bothered him for it meant he had a conscience, something he would not normally own up to.

He got out of bed, went into the bathroom and switched on the immersion heater. At the sink, he splashed water on his face, then began to shave mechanically, his attention focused on his reflected eyes, searching them for signs of betrayal.

The Mountegard tribesman: whose name had been Hanag. One of the many he had trained and lived with during his two tours in Vietnam. Hanag had died fighting the Viet Cong, and Jackson had taken the man's wife and two of his sisters as wives.

They were all dead now. He had betrayed them all. But only after they had betrayed themselves and their American allies. They were a wild people. The CIA and the Special Forces had trained them as mercenaries to fight alongside the US and South Vietnamese forces. But they had killed indiscriminately as they saw all Vietnamese, North and South, as their natural enemies. And given half the chance, they indulged their murderous instincts against the Americans. Their only interests were killing and booty, particularly gold. And Jackson and the other Americans had eventually lost control of the tribesmen.

When Nixon began the American pull-out and sued for peace, the Mountegard kept right on killing. And when American aid was finally stopped, they turned against their mentors. So Jackson, just before his recall, led his group of four hundred tribesmen into a well-prepared ambush. The artillery and napalm left the men, women and children with no chance whatsoever, and they all died horribly, his own wives included, in the last of the many, little holocausts that afflicted Vietnam during those last, tragic days.

He dabbed at the blood on his chin with a towel, then rinsed the lather from his face. He went back to the bedroom to awaken Billy, but she was already up, pulling on a pair of shorts.

'You can have a hot bath in a few minutes,' said Jackson.

Billy turned her back. 'I'm going out.' Her voice was sulky.

'What's wrong?' asked Jackson.

'Nothing,' said Billy sharply.

She put on a white T-shirt, and tried to push her way past Jackson.

'What's the matter?' demanded Jackson, holding her at the elbows at arm's length. 'Tell me.'

'You're going away again. I can tell.' She began to cry. 'You were dreaming again last night. Sweating and groaning. I can tell,' she sobbed.

He tried to smile. 'I often dream,' he protested.

'Not like that.' And she curled her body inside his arms and rested her forehead on his chest. 'You said you wouldn't have to go away again. Not after the last time.'

Jackson could feel her hot tears on his skin. He had not realised that his dream occurred just before he was about to make a trip. 'I thought so too, honey,' he said, pulling her closer to his body. She wrapped both arms round his waist. 'Maybe this will be the last time. And then I can finish for good.'

'Promise,' she asked in a little girl's voice.

'Promise. I'll only be gone for a week. Two at the outside. Just that extra bit of cash. That's all I need. Then we can both cock our noses at the cruel old world.'

III

He took a taxi to the Poste Restante to collect the envelope from Pierre, then walked down to the port. He needed the extra cash, that was why he had given himself another year working for Pierre.

When he had first come to Fuengirola, it had been a sleepy fishing village well away from the tourist resorts of Torremolinos and Marbella, a place where a man could put down roots and live out his life without any interference from outsiders. But now, the place had changed beyond recognition. Fuengirola was one of the best and most expensive resorts on the Costa del Sol.

He had been able to cope with the change, because after all, it was responsible for his meeting Billy. She had come with friends on a two-week package holiday from Manchester, and she had stayed for three years. Three of the best years he had ever had.

But it was not the influx of tourists that had made up his mind to quit the place. It was the arrival of certain types of British gentlemen with Cockney accents and plenty of money. They bought the best villas, just as he had done himself, and with their wives and girl-friends, they tried to lord it over the expatriate community. It was Billy who had first drawn his attention to their

53

arrival, and later told him that this stretch of coast had been dubbed the Costa del Crime.

The presence of the Cockney thieves was attracting the attention of the British and Spanish police. Interpol were also involved. And while there was nothing on file about Jackson in any international police records he nevertheless felt uncomfortable and worried by the constant prying and snooping of the police. It was only a matter of time before some bright officer would start to question his presence there.

He went into the *Sans Souci* and ordered a fino. It was too early in the morning for a serious drink. He had decided on Holland as their next home. But had not yet broken the news to Billy: he would do so on his return. He opened the letter from Pierre and read his instructions. First port of call was Argentina.

IV

Billy shopped like a miser in the old market. She had planned paella for lunch. Maria, her house-girl, followed in her wake, collecting the purchases as they were made and storing them in in the thermos bag she carried.

The shopping completed, Billy dismissed Maria, then set off for the Sans Souci to meet Jackson. On the way there, she made a telephone call to a local number.

'*Digame*,' said a man's voice.

'Billy,' she said. 'Tomorrow Eagle is airborne.' She hung up without waiting for a reply.

JANUARY 1985
London, England

'And your brother? Jim, isn't it?' asked Cameron.

'Yes. He's fine. I spent the New Year with him and his family,' said Mercer. He suspected that Cameron had mugged up on his file.

'Things must be bad in his line of business at the moment. As they are everywhere,' continued Cameron. They were walking along Westminster Bridge Road towards St George's Circus. Mercer had arrived at the lobby of Century House at nine-thirty, his identification badge at the ready for the security check, when Cameron had tapped him on the shoulder. He had obviously been waiting for him. He suggested Mercer would like to accompany him on a constitutional. Except for a couple of very polite good mornings when passing each other in the corridor, this was the first time that the two men had actually met for a talk.

'He's keeping his head above water. Business is bound to pick up,' said Mercer.

'Good. Good. It's the small businessman who keeps this country afloat. Always has been.' The two men parted company momentarily as a woman and her poodle commandeered the centre of the pavement. 'And that friend of yours,' said Cameron when they were reunited. 'From your Oxford days. Todd is it?'

Mercer swallowed. 'Tom Todd. Yes. He's fine, too. I don't see him all that often.'

'Not as much as you used to, eh?' said Cameron archly.

'Both too busy to let our social lives interfere with work', replied Mercer. He wondered what Cameron was driving at. Was he warning him off Todd? Or just letting him know that he knew about the leaks Mercer had made to Todd at the Old Man's instigation. What did it matter anyway? he told himself. He would be gone in March.

Cameron walked ahead. Both men wore dark overcoats against the cold, frosty chill of the morning. Only Cameron wore a hat, a brown trilby which sat squarely on his head. Even then, with the added height, he only came up to Mercer's shoulder. Mercer stooped forward slightly when he walked in the company of smaller men and was round-shouldered as a result.

Suddenly Cameron turned to the kerbside, raised an arm and waved. A black Mercedes cruised to a halt at the kerb and Cameron invited Mercer to get in. 'Close the partition, Bob,' ordered Cameron. A sheet of glass rose up from the rear of the front seats to divide the car into two halves. 'Soundproof. Bulletproof, too,' said Cameron leaning forward to tap the glass. A noisy clunk followed as the doors of the vehicle were centrally locked.

'Where're we going?' asked Mercer.

Cameron ignored the question. 'The Director and I have been reading your first draft for next month's JIC. Very detailed. Very impressive.' He nodded thoughtfully to himself as he spoke.

'Thank you,' said Mercer.

'My time in America taught me a lot. The Americans are very direct people. They don't like frills, padding, camouflage. They call a spade a spade. Everything is straight down the middle.' Cameron made the gesture with his right arm. 'Straight down the middle,' he repeated.

'Really.'

'You've seen the latest edition of Soviet Military Power?' Mercer nodded. 'The Pentagon has spent a lot of effort in putting that together. A very impressive document indeed.'

'Very,' said Mercer. He knew what was coming next.

'The Pentagon's conclusion is that the Russians are ahead of the Americans in weaponry technology. And as you know, the Pentagon derives most of its intelligence on Russian matters from satellites. What the Americans call *elint*. Electronic intelligence as opposed . . .'

'As opposed to human intelligence gathering – *humint*,' finished Mercer.

'Thank you,' said Cameron. 'So you can see my predicament.'

'I can't, you know,' said Mercer sarcastically. The car turned full circle at the Circus and went back the way they had just come.

Cameron continued unabashed. 'Very well. The NATO Alliance has deployed *Pershing* and *Cruise* missiles. And Britain, in additon, has taken *Trident*. Work has already begun on the first submarine up in, er . . .'

'Barrow-in-Furness,' said Mercer.

'Yes. Barrow. Good.' Cameron pushed his hands into his pockets. 'We've had our share of problems with the Americans over the years. Both politically, and in the field of intelligence. And as you know, the Russians have never been slow to exploit any differences between us and the Americans.'

'That's what they're in business to do,' said Mercer.

'True. And they made merry in the seventies.'

'I know. I read about it in *Time* magazine.'

Cameron sighed. 'The Americans were under a cloud then. Still licking the wounds inflicted by Nixon and Carter.'

'The Americans are their own worst enemy.'

'But times have changed,' persisted Cameron. 'A new President has been in power for four years now. He has turned the country around.'

'I read all about that in *Newsweek*.'

Cameron gave him a sour look. 'The President is determined not only to prevent the further spread of Russian influence throughout the world, but is equally determined to push it back from where it came. Back inside Russia. He's going on the offensive. Hence *Pershing* and *Cruise*.'

57

'And Britain's going along?' asked Mercer.

'The Prime Minister and the President have identical views on the matter.'

'Hence *Trident*? Britain's contribution to the offensive?'

'Precisely,' said Cameron. 'A new era of trust and co-operation. Extending to all fields, in all directions.'

'On intelligence matters, too?'

'Of course. We will be working much more closely with the American intelligence agencies, particularly the CIA,' said Cameron.

'I see,' said Mercer.

'Good. Now can you see the point I was trying to make earlier?'

'What about?' asked Mercer, being deliberately obtuse.

'Your JIC draft report. And the Pentagon's document.' He waited for Mercer to answer. He did not oblige. 'They contradict one another,' Cameron said finally.

'I know they do.' He looked out of the window. They were crossing Westminister Bridge.

'The CIA representative on the Joint Intelligence Committee would find that rather perplexing.'

'Cause problems for his direct call a spade a spade approach would it?'

'Something like that. We can hardly talk of a new era of co-operation if at the first get-together we have this glaring contradiction.'

'It's your era, not mine,' Mercer stared at Cameron. 'My draft is based on intelligence gathered by my networks inside Russia. Backed up by other sources; some from America, GCHQ and the . . .'

'I know. I know,' interjected Cameron. 'But there are too many trends. Too many guesses. Too many frills.'

'Don't forget the camcuflage.'

'The Americans like to *draw a bead* on their enemy; to see him without any of the trapping. Naked. Out there.' Cameron's arm swept across Mercer's vision. 'Your JIC draft dresses him up, disguises him.'

'So we're working for the Americans, are we?'

'Co-operating with them.'

'To the extent that we tailor-make JIC assessments to their liking.'

'Not at all,' said Cameron. 'It's a question of consistency.'

'Then tell the Pentagon to revise their document. Mine is okay.'

'As I said before, there are too many trends and guesses.'

'Oh, I give up,' said Mercer angrily. 'Just tell me what you want me to censor.' He knew he could not win against Cameron and his kind.

'Just remove as irrelevancies, not censor,' said Cameron with a smile. 'Some of the information in your draft may be of tremendous interest to demographers and social scientists, but it's hardly what I would call hard intelligence.'

'Have it your own way.'

'Okay then. Forget about rising crime rate, the disintegration of the medical and social services. A brief mention of the graft and corruption will suffice, the problems in the oil industry and the harvest. Again, a brief note should . . .'

'Most of that intelligence comes from the Central Statistical Directorate of the USSR. The Directorate feeds the Central Committee and the Politburo with it, and in turn it forms the basis of policy decisions. Sir Peter relied heavily on it for his own interpretation of what was happening inside Russia.'

'Alas, Sir Peter is no longer with us. We now have new priorities,' said Cameron smugly.

A new broom, indeed, thought Mercer. The victory of the Peterhouse Mafia. The car was now recrossing Westminister Bridge, heading back towards Century House. 'You cannot take the Russian Military in isolation and expect to get a true picture of Russia,' said Mercer as a final protest. He knew it was hopeless. 'You must look at what is happening to the people.'

'But the Americans only see Russia in one way. The

correct way. And that is as a giant military complex whose aim is the annihilation of the Western world and its way of life.' Cameron tugged a piece of fluff from the hem of his coat. 'And I don't have to remind you that I totally endorse such a perspective.'

Mercer started to speak, but Cameron interrupted him. 'I don't want to hear your litany of hard-luck stories about these poor people in Russia. I want hard facts on the Military. On budgets, on spending, research and development. No frills. No disinformation. Otherwise the Americans will laugh in our faces.'

'The Americans have all that information anyway,' said Mercer.

'Then they'll be very happy to receive confirmation of their findings from us. Won't they?'

'Why not simply write my draft yourself and get someone from Documents to sign it in my name.'

'I want you to write it. Then present it personally at the JIC meeting.'

The final humiliation, thought Mercer, for the loyalty he had shown to the Old Man. He could see that Cameron was truly enjoying himself. 'If I agree to what you want,' said Mercer. 'You'll have no further calls on me? I can pack my bags and go?'

'Of course. Of course. How does the end of March suit you?' replied Cameron benevolently.

FEBRUARY 1985
Uxbridge, England

I

Lacey parked his car in the usual place. Even though the sun was bright, there was still a bitter winter chill on the air. So he buttoned up his car-coat before collecting his hat and briefcase from the passenger seat, and climbed awkwardly out of the car onto the pavement. The departing boom of a jetliner greeted him and he flinched unconsciously as it zoomed past overhead.

He locked the car door and put on his hat, only to remove it seconds later in salute to the greying form of Mrs Hollins, who stood sentry behind the yellowing lace curtains of number seventeen. She did not acknowledge the gesture as it was only Tuesday and pay day was Friday.

He waddled across the road and turned left into the High Street, his heavy body rolling on its stumpy legs. He paid Mrs Hollins five pounds a week for the privilege of parking outside her house, which gave him a saving of almost twenty pounds over the only legitimate parking area near his photographic shop, the multi-storey hulk that towered above the precinct.

He could see it in the distance, its bulk dwarfing the neat rows of shops that lined the top end of the Street. He was satisfied with the arrangement he had with the old dear and didn't mind the walk to his shop as it afforded him the only exercise he ever had time to take; and enabled him to prepare for the first few hours of work after the trauma of driving to Uxbridge from Golders Green.

Lacey saw the man in the raincoat out of the corner of his eye as he walked past the jewellers, but he paid no attention. At the bakers, his right hand was groping in

61

his coat pocket for the heavy bunch of keys; by the delicatessen, his stubby fingers had isolated the two keys that opened the shop; and by the time he reached the front door, he had them out, pointed like a sword, aimed at the keyholes above the letterbox.

He stopped suddenly in his tracks, his right arm extended, pointing at the door. The man, the one he'd noticed window-shopping at the jewellers? He checked his watch. It was just after nine. And today was Monday? he asked himself. No. Tuesday. He'd forgotten. Damn, he swore at himself. It was Tuesday. He should have opened at eight-thirty. He shouldn't have kept him waiting like that.

He quickly unlocked the front door and pushed it open, leapt inside and crossed to the counter where he dropped his case. He went to a brown metal box on the wall behind, unlocking it with a third key which his fingers had automatically sorted, and turned off the burglar alarm. He took off his hat, pulled himself out of the car-coat, and gathered everything up and dumped it in a chair just behind the main door, which he closed with a sweep of his left foot. The bell rang.

He turned on the lights then disappeared into the back room, worry and panic, brought on by his forgetfulness, urging him on. He tugged open a cupboard under the stairwell and flicked on the light. It was empty except for two rows of shelves which were bare. He stepped inside and dropped to his knees. The button was hidden on the floor, just behind the door jamb. He pressed it.

There was a whine as the back panel of the cupboard rose into the ceiling to reveal another set of shelves on which rested several large photograph albums. He stepped back and closed the cupboard doors, and returned to the front of the shop. The man came in a few minutes later as Lacey was pulling on his white coat.

He's just going on shift, thought Lacey, and he cursed himself again for his stupidity and for keeping him hanging around unnecessarily. The man's raincoat was too small for him, and the cuffs of his dark blue uniform peeked out, showing a couple of silver buttons. The man smiled at Lacey, feeling unsure of himself, looking obviously worried by the uncharacteristic lapse on Lacey's part.

'Traffic,' said Lacey, and waved the man into the back room. He went, relief showing on his face. Lacey collected his mail from the wire basket on the back of the front door and was still sorting through it some fifteen minutes later when the man re-emerged, pulling on his coat. He stood in front of the counter.

Lacey looked around, his head bobbing hither and thither, until he located his briefcase on the chair, partly hidden by his coat. He pointed. 'Could you pass me my case?' The man turned, following the finger. 'On the chair.'

He retrieved the case and carried it across to Lacey, who opened it with the care of a miser opening his wallet. He fumbled around inside before taking out a bundle of photographic envelopes neatly secured by several thick elastic bands. He fanned the bundle slowly until he saw the one he wanted, which he pulled free and handed over to the man. 'Mister Wilson,' he said patronisingly, to hide his embarrassment and annoyance. Wilson took the envelope and slid it into an inside pocket without inspecting the contents.

'Thanks,' said Wilson. 'I'll see you in a fortnight, if not before.' Lacey nodded, returning the bundle to his briefcase. 'I can make it nine o'clock if that's better for you.'

Lacey considered for a moment before dismissing it. 'No. We will stick to eight-thirty,' he replied, reasserting himself.

'Fine with me. Be seeing you, Mister Lacey.' Wilson left, the chime of the bell drowning Lacey's farewell.

An occasional shopper peered in the window, inspecting the array of cameras and accessories, but none ventured inside to inquire further. After a while, Lacey made his way into the back room again. Half way in, he stopped, his face reddening with anger. 'Lazy bastard,' he said loudly as he saw two of the portrait books from the cupboard lying open on the table.

He marched over to the table and looked down at the books. From the open pages, two faces stared blankly up at him, one of them a woman's, blurred and almost indistinct, taken, he guessed, at long range in poor light.

He read through the legend below it, saw the names the woman habitually used, then turned the page as the story continued. 'Bitch,' he said, as he finished and snapped the book closed. He carried it back to the cupboard and put it back on one of the shelves. He saw that Wilson had also been busy with several of the other books, as they were no longer in the order he had previously left them.

He collected the other album from the table and shelved it, before closing down the back panel and refastening the cupboard door. At least Wilson had made the effort and had actually taken the portrait books out and inspected them. Some of the others, he knew, just went through the motions: they sat in the backroom and twiddled their thumbs for fifteen minutes before coming back into the shop to claim their money. Wilson was probably one of the better ones, he concluded. But lazy also. And he paid scant regard to security in leaving the books lying around like that. Lacey would have to speak to him about that when he called again.

II

He filled the kettle and plugged it in. He could understand Wilson's position: it wasn't the best job in the world. It was boring, standing there for ten or twelve hours continually, watching and waiting for faces that may never appear. But it paid well and there were few risks.

Wilson was one of those silent, faceless people who crowd behind crash barriers at international airports, where incoming passengers first emerge from the frustrations of immigration and customs, holding signs, boards or placards on which are scrawled the names of individuals or companies. But Wilson and his kind never actually meet anybody from arrivals. They just hang about all day and night with their boards. Watching and waiting.

Watching for the faces that appeared in Lacey's albums. Watching and inspecting every face that, in Wilson's case, passed through Heathrow's terminals. Faces in the portrait books: some blurred, some sharp and exact, others grainy and indistinct, copied from old prints and newspapers. All neatly filed and catalogued. All the faces with a legend, all with a story to tell. Tales of violence and death put together by the biographers of Mossad.

These albums were duplicated many times over, available for inspection in many little shops and contact points like Lacey's, all close to international airports. And men like Wilson had their counterparts worldwide. All in the pay of Mossad. All watching and looking. Searching for the faces of terrorism.

All factions of the Palestinian terrorist movement were represented in the books. They were the men and women most sought after by the Israelis. Their allies too, the Libyans, the Japanese, the Italians and Germans. As well as some Basques, Irishmen and many Americans. In short anyone who posed a threat. These were the people most hostile to Israel and had proved it by many acts of murder and mayhem. They were all under sentence of death.

Since the unsuccessful attempt on the life of Israel's Ambassador to Britain, Shlomo Argov, in the summer of '82, by a squad of Abu Nidal's Palestinians, Israeli security throughout the world had been increased to such an extent that very few countries did not have a representative or an agent of Mossad somewhere monitoring the movements in and around international frontiers and entry points.

Lacey made himself a cup of tea. He had never been involved in an identification and doubted if he would ever be. In any case that was not part of his job. He simply provided up-to-date pictures and stories for men like Wilson. It was their job to be ready for the appearance of one of those faces at the barriers and to make it known to the Mossad men at the airport. He sipped his tea. He wondered who held the portrait books at Gatwick. Was there a set at Luton? Manchester? Who looked after them?

He took his tea back into the shop. His speculations were rudely interrupted by the clang of the bell announcing his first genuine customer of the day, an harrassed mother with two crying offspring in tow. He beamed a welcome to the woman who just scowled at him, while the two children buried themselves in the folds of her coat.

MARCH 1985
Godalming, England

I

'Forty love,' said Cameron.

'If you say so,' mumbled Mercer, walking back to the base-line. He was freezing and his only thought was to get the stupid game over as quickly as possible so that he could soak in a nice hot bath. Who ever heard of tennis in the middle of bloody March? he thought to himself.

Cameron sent down the next service to Mercer's backhand. Mercer didn't move his feet, and his racket was too finely angled. He skyed the ball which landed on his side of the net. 'Game,' announced Cameron with finality and strode to the sideline. Mercer joined him, and, for the umpteenth time that morning thought how ridiculous he looked in his tennis whites, which were only one shade lighter than his exposed arms and legs. Cameron, by contrast, superbly tanned and fit, looked the part, brimming with health and vitality: he had been bouncing round the court from the opening service, like some latter-day Chuck McKinley, reliving his Wimbledon triumph of '63.

'Four games to love, Joe,' said Cameron wiping the sweat from his forehead with a towel. The racket handle received the same treatment. Mercer stood idly by, shivering. 'And one set to love.'

'I'm still warming up,' said Mercer.

'You're out of practice. And out of condition.' Cameron adjusted the sweat bands on his wrists. 'I played every day back in the States. Indoors in the winter, of course.'

'Of course,' intoned Mercer. Then why aren't we playing indoors now? he thought, and stamped his racket onto the clay of the court. He picked up two loose balls as he walked back to the service-line. He served a double fault which brought forth a grim head shake from Cameron. Mercer retrieved the balls and served again, low down into the net. His next service was weak and short, barely creeping over the net and bouncing tamely at Cameron's feet as he came in to meet it. He knocked it away with a savage forehand.

Mercer was love thirty and heading for defeat, when Cameron, trying to pull Mercer into the game by returning a soft service with an equally weak shot from the base-line, was caught out by Mercer's unintended drop shot that came off the wood, forcing Cameron to dash to the net where he slipped and fell as he strove to reach the ball which had just completed its second bounce. He cut his knee on the roughened court and retired to the side to dab away the blood with his towel. His immaculate white shorts were dirty and had split on one side. Mercer remained where he was, looking round at the scenery, trying to hide his amusement.

The game went to deuce as Cameron limped his way around the court and Mercer finally clinched it when Cameron, with a pained expression and an audible gasp, was taken in by Mercer's drop shot off the wood again. Mercer was feeling a lot better. 'One-four,' said Mercer happily.

'Four-one,' growled Cameron. 'I'm serving.' And serve he did. Mercer's triumph was short-lived. Cameron put in four first services, only one of which Mercer managed to return over the net, and then it was too long, bouncing out by a good two yards.

They changed ends again. Cameron's limp seemed to have disappeared as he bobbed and danced on the base-line ready to receive. It put Mercer off and he did not manage a point throughout. Nor did Cameron try to bring him into the game by repeating his generosity: he smashed away all Mercer's effort with a cool, hardened precision. 'Game, set and match,' he shouted rather loudly.

Mercer saw the reason. Mary Binder. She was coming towards them from the house, smiling brightly. 'You two finished already?' she asked. Mercer noted she was suitably attired for the cold morning in a camel coat which was tied at the waist and her feet were clad in long suede boots topped with fur. On her head she wore a thick woollen scarf that completely hid her auburn hair and made her face into an oval. She was without make-up and her eyes, a dark brown, sparkled with light amusement. 'I take it the game went to form.'

'Joe needs to get himself fit,' said Cameron.

'Not used to these high-technology rackets,' said Mercer.

Mary Binder linked an arm through Cameron's. 'If it's not his own equipment then it's somebody's else's that's to blame for his poor performances,' she said with a shake of her head. 'Let's go for a walk.' She led Cameron off around the court and out through the gap in the hedge towards the orchard. Mercer stood and watched them until they disappeared, then slowly went back into the house.

His room was on the attic floor away from the other guests, up a flight of stairs that creaked and moaned at every footfall. An old fashioned double bed with brass bedsteads left just enough space for a rickety plywood wardrobe into which Mercer had placed the contents of his weekend bag. He stripped off his tennis whites that Cameron had lent him and put on his dressing-gown that hung over the edge of the unmade bed. He collected a towel and walked down to the bathroom next to Mary Binder's room.

The water was piping hot and he filled the bath as much as he dared before gingerly edging into it to thaw out. The rising steam quickly clouded the window and mirror. He had not seen Mary for two or three months. Rumour had it that Cameron was spending a lot of time in the squat annexe building that housed the history of the Service. But Mercer paid scant attention to such gossip. Cameron's wife was still back in the States trying to sell the family home with the able assistance of Jimmy Hunter, formerly Cameron's deputy, and now his replacement. In more ways than one, thought Mercer, if the whispers were correct.

He soaked himself for half an hour then climbed out just as he heard a babble of voices down below; the intrepid horsemen, led by Leonard Binder, Mary's brother, returning after their early morning gallop. 'A weekend in the country. A little fun, a little business,' was how Cameron had issued the invitation. 'Sherwood needs a lift down,' was Cameron's way of saying that a refusal was unacceptable. So Mercer had obeyed his master's voice and had arrived at the Edwardian mansion just outside Godalming late on the Friday night. Most of the other house guests had already gone to bed, and Mercer and Sherwood had been left on their own when Cameron, with a yawn, decided to do likewise.

Mercer returned to his room and dressed wondering when the fun was going to get under way. He had been rudely awakened by Cameron at seven and given the option of horses or tennis. He chose the latter because in his student days he had always fancied himself as another Rod Laver. He should have guessed that whatever options Cameron should offer, they would certainly be ones at which Cameron excelled.

Leonard Binder's wife, Susan, was laughing her horsey laugh as Mercer joined the gathering in the morning-room. She was dressed in fawn jodhpurs with a matching roll-neck sweater underneath a dark tan body-warmer. She carried her riding hat in one hand and was slashing at the air with the other one which held her riding-crop. 'The bloody woman kept whipping the poor beast. In the end I had to get Leonard to take over.'

'I managed to get the crop from her. And I swear she would have used her feet if her husband hadn't shown up at that moment. But one word from him and it was all over,' said Leonard Binder.

'Is he a prince?' asked Mary Binder.

'They're all Princes. Give them an acre of sand and a few servants, and it's Prince-this, Sheik-that,' said Susan Binder in disgust. 'Anyway, the horses are still at the stables, but they haven't been down for weeks.' Mercer had heard the story before. The Binders ran an equestrian establishment in Sussex and they had tried to cash in on the current fashion, the British-based Arabs and their seemingly endless supply of hard currency. But the Binders had been saddled with an Arab and his wife who still adhered to the basic tenets of Mohamed's teaching. The wife wore the black chador over her riding breeches and refused to remove her veil to accommodate her hard hat. Susan's attempts to mount her on a horse had finally ended with the animal shying away, and the woman attacking it with her whip.

'Breakfast, anybody?' asked Cameron as the conversation flagged. He was still parading around in his blood-stained tennis clothes. He spotted Mercer by the door and winked at him. 'Follow me, then,' he said after receiving several nods, and he led the exodus across the hall into the breakfast-room. Simmons, the man hired as chief cook and bottle washer for the weekend, was just putting the finishing touches to the ladened table. 'I could eat a horse,' he said dismissing Simmons with a wave of his hand.

'Not one of mine,' said Leonard Binder. 'Too old and tough.' His humour was rewarded by a poke in the ribs from his spouse.

II

Mercer made up a desultory fourth at bridge that evening, partnering Ronnie Fisher against the Binders in a game that was notable for its low scoring and flamboyant bidding. The conversation was equally as extreme though Mercer did most of the listening. He was more interested in what had happened to Mary Binder. She seemed to have disappeared.

Leonard Binder introduced farming into the conversation right after the opening bid, fascinating his audience with details of last year's cereal crop production and what was expected of this year's crop.

More farming facts were dealt around the table as the game progressed. Occasionally Fisher would introduce some aspects of City finance into the conversation as that was where his interest lay. But the Binders always managed to steer the talk back to farming or horses. At the end of the evening, Mercer felt as if he was up to his knees in horse muck and silage.

He called it a night at ten o'clock. He was tired after the afternoon's walk. Forced march more like, he told himself as he left the Library. He had commented during the hike to Sherwood that Cameron had achieved a great deal in furnishing the house so well in the short time he had been home from the States. 'It was his mother's house,' Sherwood had answered. 'She died a couple of years ago and it has stood empty till now.'

The television was on in the lounge, and the door was ajar. Mercer could hear the sound of a football commentary coming from within, and above it, Cameron's voice. 'In America, there's seating for everybody in the stadiums. None of this standing nonsense.' Mercer continued along the corridor to the kitchen. Simmons wasn't there. He made himself a cup of hot chocolate and carried it up to his room without encountering anybody. Before falling asleep, he decided that Cameron had everything going for him.

III

He woke with a start. Had he been groaning in his sleep? There it was again. The creaking noise. The central-heating did not extend to this corner of the house and

Mercer was reluctant to expose his arm to the cold night air to reach over to the bedside table to turn on the light. The creaking grew louder. Somebody was coming up the stairs to his room. He could not see his watch face, but he thought it was after midnight at least. The door opened. Mercer could make out a black shape, huddled and bent. It moved towards him.

'Move over,' said Mary Binder impatiently. 'A girl could freeze to death up here.' Something slithered from her shoulders and fell to the floor. Mercer moved over into the cooler part of the bed. Mary Binder snuggled into the warmer half. Her thigh was cold as it touched Mercer's. He lay on his back. She thumped him in the chest. 'Bastard,' she said.

'Why?' said Mercer.

'Why haven't you been over to see me? Called me, even?'

'I've been busy.'

She thumped him in the chest again. 'Have you turned into a monk? Or have you tired of my charms, kind sir?' Her right hand, cold and smooth, began to move upwards inside his thigh. Mercer's breath caught momentarily in the back of his throat. 'No. And no.' She bent over him. The bed groaned. 'But I've been hearing rumours.'

'About Alex and myself?' Mercer nodded. She laughed.

'What's so funny? The way you've been playing up to him all day I should think there's some substance to all the talk.'

'Don't be so pompous, Joe. And if there's any truth to the rumours then it's all your fault. I'm not a nun you know.' She bounced over onto her back. The bed shuddered.

'Ssshh,' hushed Mercer. 'You'll wake the whole house. If your creeping up here hasn't woken everybody already.'

'Then at least there'll be some truth to any gossip that comes from this weekend,' she said tartly.

'Okay. Okay. There's nothing between you and Cameron.'

'I didn't say that exactly.' Mercer sat up on his elbow. She was laughing behind her hand which was cupped over her mouth. Mercer pulled it away. 'Sorry Joe. Couldn't resist the little barb.' She reached up her arms and encircled his neck. 'When I go to bed with a man, I like to make love. Not take part in a horizontal jogging session.'

'So you have been to bed with him?' said Mercer.

'Just once.'

'Why?' Her arms pulled his face closer to hers as she shrugged. 'Doesn't matter,' Mercer said finally.

'I thought I liked him. He's handsome. Attentive. Good company.'

'All the things I'm not.'

'Don't be silly, Joe. You're all those things.'

'Am I?'

She took her arms away and began to stroke his chest. 'I don't know what it is about you but you seem to be in a world of your own half the time. I can't really explain it. It's as if you've no life of your own. You use other people, dropping in here and there, joining in their lives, making them your own. Then move on. Elsewhere. Other people. Other lives.' She paused and Mercer realised she was upset. He kissed her gently on the cheek. 'Why didn't you call me?'

'Is that why you slept with him?'

'Yes. No. What does it matter? Why do you care?'

'I care,' he said.

'Oh I know you do.' She kissed him back. 'It's just that you have a funny way of showing it.'

'Just once?' asked Mercer.

'And that was once too many.' She giggled. 'I couldn't stand all that suppressed breathing, trying to show what a perfect specimen of manhood he is.' She began to scratch her nails along the inside of his thighs and her lips nuzzled the lobe of his ear as her tongue, wet and pointed, darted into the earhole. Her nails glided across his scrotum, and his stomach was suffused with a tingling glow which ran downwards to fill his penis.

He brought his hand across her body and nipped a nipple between finger and thumb. Her breath came quicker, hotter and she writhed and twisted as his lips found the other nipple. She rubbed his glans and he felt his own wetness spill forth. She pulled his head up and their lips met, forming a seal, and they breathed heavily into each other, slowly at first, then gaining pace, as their excitement rose. He pushed her legs apart and entered her with his fingers. She arched her back and squeezed his penis and he groaned as he rolled on top of her. She struggled against him as he knelt between her legs but she guided him inside.

IV

Lunch, beef and ham sandwiches, was served at one. Dinner was set for seven. Cameron had arranged for the women to go over to Winkworth Arboretum after lunch. Simmons would drive them in the Land Rover. Though what delights awaited them there at this time of the year Mercer could not imagine. The fun was now over. It was business from now on. Fordyce arrived at two o'clock in a chauffeur-driven Mercedes and Cameron took him immediately into the Library where they remained closeted for twenty minutes. Then Cameron returned to the Lounge where Mercer and the others were passing the time speculating about Fordyce's arrival. 'Follow me,' ordered Cameron. They went into the Library.

'Good afternoon, gentlemen,' said Fordyce.
'Good afternoon, sir,' came the chorused reply.

The seating was arranged in an arc in front of a huge mahogany desk, on the left of which sat Fordyce in a leather armchair. Cameron took up his place behind the desk as everyone sat down. It was his show. Mercer was reminded of a seminar at a university.

Cameron slowly perused the arc of faces. 'Earlier this year,' he began in a low voice. 'While visiting one of our European Stations a member of the Soviet Politburo made personal contact with me. Since then, I have had two further contacts with him.'

'To what purpose?' asked Sherwood, who was in charge of the Service's purse strings. The Treasury were forever on his back seeking to curb what they considered profligate overspending on the part of Her Majesty's Secret Service. Whenever there was a hint that more money was required by one of the Sections for something that fell outside the official budget, then Sherwood could be found haunting that particular Section. Mercer liked him very much. He was unafraid of titles and positions. He was accountable for the financing of the Service, and he expected others to be accountable for their own particular field of enterprise, especially when it came down to money. 'Defection?'

'Eventually,' answered Cameron. 'At the moment, he would prefer to work for us.'

'We would be buying information from him? Or is there a more altruistic reason for his willingness to work for us?' Sherwood was already counting the cost of such a high level source of information.

Cameron held up his hands. 'All will become clear in a few minutes, Tim. Just let me finish.' He gave a half-hearted laugh. Sherwood, thought Mercer, was stealing Cameron's thunder. 'On the third contact, I was supplied with certain intelligence which is currently undergoing evaluation both here and in America. Of course, the source has not been made known to our people. Or the Americans.'

'Gentlemen,' said Fordyce sternly. 'One of the reasons I called this meeting down here was that it could be conducted informally, in a relaxed atmosphere after enjoying a couple of days of Alex's hospitality. And, need I say,' he added, searching Mercer's face for signs of rebellion, 'without the intrusion of office politics.'

76

Cameron continued as if there had been no interruption. 'Preliminary indications are that the material is of the highest quality and that the man is who he says he is.'

'You're not sure who he is exactly?' asked Sherwood incredulously.

'I have seen him on three separate occasions – alone – and have matched his physical likeness with several photographs from our archives. The name he gave me also matches up. However, it's not beyond the realms of possibility that he is part of some clever Russian plant. He may bear a strong resemblance to the man whose name he is using. A double in fact. It will be the quality of the information that he provides that will determine whether he is the genuine article or not.' Sherwood nodded his understanding. 'As I said, indications are that he is genuine. A member of the Politburo.'

'What's his name?' asked Mercer. As Head of Russia Section, albeit for only a few more weeks, he thought he had the right to ask the question which he could see was already forming on several pairs of lips. Including the Premier, there was a baker's dozen in the Politburo. He was curious to find out who was changing his colours.

Fordyce spoke. 'Not even I know his name.' He received a few raised eyebrows for his contribution. 'His code name, however, is a different matter.'

'*Cedar*,' said Cameron. 'And the operation to control *Cedar* will be known as Janus.'

Mercer, like the others, was having difficulty switching his attention from Cameron to Fordyce and back again, as the double act went through its paces. It reminded him of a ventriloquist show, but he was unsure who had his hand up whose back.

'And even then *Cedar's* identity will be on a need to know basis,' said Cameron. 'At our first meeting, *Cedar* specifically requested that I keep his name to myself. Understandable really, when you consider that the introductory phase is usually the most insecure.'

'When Alex informed me of his contact and *Cedar's* request, I, of course, agreed to go along,' said Fordyce.

'Are we to finance Janus?' asked Sherwood.

'The Cabinet Office have agreed a special supplementary budget to finance Janus. No need to worry over that matter, Tim,' said Cameron. 'I will be working on my own with *Cedar* on all operational procedures which will be mutually agreed upon. When we are both satisfied that all is satisfactory, then I will hand over to you gentlemen. However, should *Cedar* ask for personal contact during any phase of the operation, then that will be my province.'

Mercer looked along at his companions; Sherwood of Finance; Binder, Head of Section for the Eastern Bloc; Fisher for Operations; Rushton from Evaluation and Interpretation; Peterson from Liaison. And himself, Head of Russia Section. All top people, he thought. To service a member of Soviet Politburo? He voiced his thought. 'How did *Cedar* make the initial contact?' asked Mercer.

'I can't go into specific detail at this stage. But it was a walk in,' replied Cameron. 'Surprising, isn't it?'

Miraculous, thought Mercer. Some Second Secretary for Commerce from a Russian Embassy might contemplate a walk-in into a Western Embassy or Diplomatic Mission as a prelude to defection. But a Politburo member? In Europe? Surrounded by bodyguards wherever he goes? He crossed one leg over the other and stared at the tip of his shoe. It was scuffed and unpolished. He raised his foot slightly. The heel had worn down to a wedge. He needed a new pair. Or a good cobbler.

Fordyce continued talking, but Mercer was not listening. He was deep in thought. He vaguely heard the roar of the Land Rover returning with the women, and when the meeting finally broke up before six-thirty, he left the Library without speaking to anyone, and returned to his room to change for dinner.

V

'Anything I should know about?' asked Mary, pulling herself free from his arms.

'What?' said Mercer, drowsily.

'Cameron's big meeting this afternoon, of course.'

'You know better than that,' admonished Mercer.

'Well it's certainly had an effect on you.' She got out of bed and picked up her thin dressing gown. She pulled it on and fastened it.

'Where are you going?' he asked.

'Back to my own room for a good night's rest. I'm wasting my time here.' She walked out of the room. Mercer heard the creaking boards mark her descent.

He lay down again. 'Sorry,' he whispered into the dark. He tried to sleep but couldn't. He should have pushed Cameron and *Cedar* from his mind when Mary had crept into the room just after midnight, but found it impossible. His love-making had been mechanical and distant, and Mary had felt it. Now she was upset again. He would have to make it up to her, go and see her. Perhaps send her some flowers. He had to. She must have swallowed her pride in coming to him the night before. He owed it to her and to himself to make the first move this time.

London, England

I

Mercer was deep in thought. What was nagging at him? Disbelief? Or was it envy? A Politburo member wants to work for the Service? Doesn't want to defect? Walks in off the street? Right out of the blue? Stranger things have happened in the murky intelligence world. But into whose hands falls this astounding offer? Alex Cameron's. Why him? He'd never worked in Russia or Europe. Why had *Cedar* chosen him? He was in the right place at the right time? *Cedar* had heard of him from sources inside America, perhaps, and knew him as a man to be trusted? Of all people, it would have to be Cameron.

He walked over to the plate-glass window that gave a soundless view over Westminster Bridge Road but did not look out: there was something vaguely disconcerting about the streams of noiseless traffic creeping along the carriageways, close enough to see, but apparently too far away to hear. *Cedar* and Janus: the whole affair just didn't hang together. It made him uneasy. He had time on his hands and intended doing some surreptitious checking of his own. Disbelief? Envy? The two motives faced each other, like a pair of muddy crocodiles on opposite sides of a river bank, hungrily eyeing an approaching meal, wary and watchful, waiting to see into whose territory the victim would fall.

Leonard Binder put his head round the door. 'Busy, Joe?' he asked. Mercer waved him to come in. Binder closed the door and stood with his back to it, both hands on the doorknob. Mercer went and sat on the edge of his desk.

'What can I do for you, Leonard?' said Mercer. Binder glanced round the room quickly. He was a hoverer and a

percher. Mercer had purposefully sat on the desk because
he knew that was one of Binder's favourite perches and
that once installed, he was very difficult to uproot.
Binder settled in front of the standard light just inside
the door, then moved across the floor to the grey filing
cabinet next to the window.

'Did you enjoy the weekend?' he asked. 'Susan and I
had a wonderful time. Mary too.' He leant against the
cabinet. 'She sends her regards by the way.'

'Susan?'

'Mary, of course. Says you weren't feeling too good
Sunday evening. Couldn't stand up or something. Is that
right? You don't look too well you know.'

'Overdid it a bit with the tennis and the hike,' said
Mercer. 'I'm feeling a lot better today, despite the red
eyes.' He had driven back from Godalming first thing in
the morning and gone to the office after a brief stopover
at his flat for a shower and change of clothing. He was
tired and the muscles in his legs ached with stiffness.
Yes, flowers for Mary, he thought.

Binder had moved again. 'Great. Smashing,' he said
with his back to Mercer, as he perused the book shelf.
'What do you think it was all about, Joe?' He faced
Mercer. 'Cameron's little meeting yesterday?' He was
frowning.

'I thought it was quite straight-forward, Leonard.
Didn't you?' Most of Binder's questions were loaded.
Mercer knew what he was after.

'Yes,' said Binder slowly and cupped his chin in his
right hand. 'But why you and me? Why were we included?'
Back to the filing cabinet.

Mercer stood up. What Binder wanted was confirmation that Mercer was indeed leaving the Service.
With Mercer gone, Binder, in all probability, would move
up to Head of Russia Section. 'Didn't Cameron say that
we're to be part of the team which would service *Cedar*?'

'Yes he did.'

'But in what capacity?' Binder looked meaningfully at

Mercer. 'Would you be on the team?' Mercer shook his head. 'Your resignation's still in, is it?'

'Yes it is.'

Relief flooded Binder's face. 'They're trying to persuade you to stay? Fordyce and Cameron?'

'On the contrary, Leonard,' said Mercer.

He frowned again. 'Strange.' He raised his eyes to the ceiling. 'Then why brief you on *Cedar*?' he said after a pause.

'That's a question I'd very much like the answer to myself, Leonard. It's been bothering me ever since Sunday night.'

II

It was rumoured that Douglas Carvey could fly around the world for less than the price of dinner for two at the Savoy. Some said he had actually done so, just to prove the point, returning dusty and dishevelled after a journey lasting twelve days, still wearing the same clothes he had set off in. He had once been the owner of one of the first bucket shops in the West End, and there wasn't an airline, a timetable or an airport, that had not fallen under his patient scrutiny. He was a careful, precise man in his early sixties, and was in charge of the Travel Section for the Service.

He was careful about his budget, precise in his timetabling of journeys and prissy with his female staff about recording all transactions between Travel and the other Service Sections. He organised and ran his Section like an airline schedule in reverse, arriving each morning for work at nine and leaving precisely at five. His staff were compelled to follow his example.

Mercer was somewhat surprised, therefore, to find Mrs Warburton still beavering away at her desk when he strode into Travel that evening at six o'clock. But he had come prepared. He carried a bunch of papers and chitties and explained to Mrs Warburton that he had to check through some of his Section's expenses as one or two of his people had been wayward in submitting their accounts.

'November through to March did you say?' asked Mrs Warburton. Mercer said yes. She went to the shelf behind her desk and pulled down five black ledgers. Mercer moved in to help her, and they carried the ledgers to a spare desk.

'Spot of overtime?' asked Mercer as he sat down to work.

'Two of the girls are on holiday and I'm trying to make inroads into the backlog.' She went back to her desk.

Carvey did not allow overtime. Nor did he approve of his staff staying late to catch up on work. Yet he would not accept any excuses if the paperwork was not up to date. Mercer opened the first ledger. Except for the signature column, all the handwriting belonged to Mrs Warburton. He had seen it often enough, a neat, exact hand, in the favoured green ink; she wrote all her memos, reprimands and complaints in longhand.

Nobody could travel abroad on Service business from Century House without first going through the Travel Section. Not even the Director or his Deputy were immune, though they were usually spared having to collect and sign for their tickets and documentation, that duty being extended to their secretaries. Everyone else had to sign personally, alongside the date and day of travel, the destination, the cost of the fare and the expected return date, all of which had been entered in the record by Mrs Warburton when her booking clerk had finalised all the arrangements and collected the tickets from whichever airline had been selected by the careful Mr Carvey.

From time to time during his search of the records, Mercer kept up his pretence by scribbling a few words on some of the papers he had brought with him. He ran his eye down the pages, looking at dates, names and destinations, the record of the travelling arrangements of

Service personnel. He spotted his own name only once, an aborted trip to Paris early in November. He saw Cameron's name four times in all.

He double-checked. Mrs Warburton had finished and was waiting for him to do likewise. He hurried through the last days of February. Nothing else caught his eye. It had taken him an hour. He replaced the ledgers himself and then walked Mrs Warburton to the lift. They said good-night. Mercer thanked her again. He walked down two flights of stairs to the Duty Officer's room. He needed to be absolutely sure.

III

Alan Bland was on duty. Mercer made two cups of coffee while Alan droned on about his garden and the prospects of Yorkshire Cricket Club in the coming season. He was nearing retirement; grey-haired with a chestnut complexion. He thought only of the time he would have to spend on the cultivation of his precious roses. He was far too casual about who wandered in and out of the Duty Room. But for once, Mercer was glad of it. Bland talked on and on and Mercer listened and smiled, nodding when he thought it appropriate while he examined the logs for Heathrow and Gatwick. The Service's men at the major international airports logged their fellow officers in and out of the country. Cameron's name appeared four times in the Heathrow record. But not in the Gatwick one. He glanced through the log for military flights from Brise Norton just in case Cameron had used that method to get to Europe. He had not.

Bland did not seem to notice Mercer leaving for he was still chatting as Mercer closed the door behind himself. He made his way home by tube. So Cameron had made four trips to Europe since his return from America – two in January to Paris and Berlin. In February he had flown to Geneva and Vienna. They had been his final destinations as there was no record of onward flights having been booked or arranged. Mrs Warburton would have known about them otherwise.

At the briefing, Cameron had said he had met three times with *Cedar*. The intial approach must therefore have been made in Paris or Berlin. Mercer favoured Berlin. Another strange aspect of the *Cedar* affair occurred to him as he left the train. Would a Politburo member have the time and the opportunity to travel outside Russia three times in less that two months? Without arousing suspicion. He did not think so.

As he came out of the Underground at Baker Street, his attention was attracted by a brightly lit advertisement: Say it with flowers said the board. He'd forgotten to send a bouquet to Mary. He went to a phone box and called the delicatessen in Ealing.

IV

'A letter,' said the old Pole, wheezing and coughing as he got to his feet. Mercer nodded. 'A letter.' Jan Oleszewski shuffled across to the bureau and pulled down the leaf. 'To our friends, no doubt.'

'Yes,' said Mercer. He produced a piece of paper from his pocket. The Pole put on his glasses and took the paper. He held it close up to his face and Mercer could see his lips moving as he read. The strains of a Gilbert and Sullivan operetta floated into the attic from downstairs where Oleszewski's family lived. He had nothing to do any more with the delicatessen on the ground floor, which was now run by his two sons, Kris and Adam. He preferred to live up here, alone, dreaming in exile of his native Poland.

Oleszewski pulled a wooden chair up to the bureau and sat down. He re-read the letter, then took up a pen and began to write slowly. From time to time he would refer to the original, his lips moving all the time.

When he had finished he put both letters side by side and studied them carefully. Satisfied that the translation was correct, he took a plain white envelope out of one of the cubby holes and wrote the address from memory. He folded the paper and tucked it inside, and licked the flap. 'Here,' he said without turning round. Mercer stood over the man, who was rummaging in a drawer. 'A twenty zloty stamp is what you need.' He found one and gave it to Mercer.

'Thanks,' said Mercer. He put the envelope and the original in his pocket.

'When I'm gone that will be the end. My sons have no heart for all this.' He waved his hand round the room. The walls were covered with the faded photographs of the Polish Government in exile, the men who had fled to Britain in '39, and who had died still believing they represented the Polish nation.

'I'll probably be gone before you, Jan,' said Mercer sadly.

V

Early Friday afternoon and Mercer was lounging in his chair, his feet up on the desk feeling very pleased with himself. Contented even. The flowers had done the trick. Mary had called him at home to thank him, and they had arranged a date for Saturday. He was looking forward to it. He pulled his desk diary into his lap and opened it. The last day of March was ringed in red. He stretched over for a pen and crossed it out. Cameron had asked him to stay on until the end of April, and Mercer had said yes. It fitted into his plans. Dermott Whelan would not be going back to Poland until next week, so Mercer could not expect a reply to his letter much before the end of April. And he wanted to be still in the Service's employ when he got to the bottom of the *Cedar* affair. His curiosity and suspicion was like an itch that refused to be satisfied.

Dermott was a good man, he thought. He had worked

for brother Jim back in Liverpool as a driver. He had saved up enough money to buy his own unit, and had then moved down to London where the prospects were better. Jim had mentioned him to Mercer on one of Mercer's infrequent trips back home when he had been stationed in Warsaw. Jim's contracts as an independent often took him to Poland and East Germany and Mercer had used him several times as a courier and postman. Unofficially. Dermott was grateful for the extra cash and never asked questions. He was street-wise and cautious, and called Mercer Mr Smith even though he knew who he really was.

The Polish letter would answer Mercer's doubts. Despite the vast censorship networks in the communist countries, there was insufficient manpower to examine all the mail that passed through the postal services. It was true that international post was subject to the prying eyes of the censors; even that which moved between towns and cities inside an individual country did not escape attention, but internal letters and mail within a city or town was free from examination. The Service used local postal services as the simplest and most direct way of passing on instructions and information to its agents behind the Iron Curtain.

Mercer's Polish wasn't very good and he lacked the practice necessary to maintain fluency. Jan Oleszewski had helped him before with messages. The man who would receive the letter was part of a ring of patriotic Poles who had frequent access to Russia. Mercer had set them up from Moscow where their business interests took them as salesmen and minor communist party functionaries. Their only concern was the overthrow of the Polish Communist Government and they used the Western Intelligence agencies indiscriminately to that end. The group was always willing to help.

The telephone rang and disturbed Mercer's meanderings. He sat upright to answer it, sliding his feet off the desk as he did so. It was Mrs Engleton. Fordyce requested his presence immediately. Urgently. He hung up and put on his jacket. He would not let Fordyce get to him and destroy his contentment. He left his office and took the lift to the top floor. Later when he recalled the feelings and events of that afternoon, he would describe himself as smugness itself. He saw the troubles that beset him as just deserts for allowing himself to get carried away by his own minor victories and would liken himself to a passenger on the Titanic.

APRIL 1985
Warsaw, Poland

There was not a lot of room for the two of them in the cramped sleeping place behind the driver's cab. They both sat on the sleeping bag, legs outstretched, to pull on their jeans and socks, then they knelt to dress the upper half of their bodies. The rain had stopped.

Dermott had fallen asleep to the rattle of rain drops on the roof of the cab and had awoken to the gentle, childish snoring of Irena, curled up in a ball with her head buried in his armpit. She was only seventeen and this was the fourth time she had stayed with him on his overnight stay in Warsaw. The confinement of the single sleeping bag meant that Irena had come awake as Dermott had moved his arm to check the time. The luminous dial on his wrist told him that it was nearly dawn, and already he could hear the slam of doors echoing throughout the lorry park.

He finished dressing first and climbed into the driver's seat. He then reached down for his small holdall, a plastic airline bag, and pulled out a blue Thermos flask and a metal cup. He poured two cups of lukewarm coffee. Irena joined him a few moments later, tying a scarf round her head, covering her short black hair that she kept in a page-boy cut because she knew Dermott like it like that.

They sat in the cab drinking their coffee, looking out of the rain-covered windscreen of the Volvo at the fleet of juggernauts neatly parked opposite. The yellow glow from the street lamps percolated through the wispy mist of the early morning that drifted in, low and heavy, from the Vistula. The tarmac, black and shiny, littered with puddles, softened the footfalls of the departing women, Irena's companions.

Dermott finished his drink and put away the flask. Irena leant backwards into the sleeping bay for her shoulder bag, opened it and took out the Max Factor make-up case that Dermott had given her. She left the ten pound note where it was, securely tucked away in the mirror compartment. She touched Dermott on the elbow then leant across and kissed him lightly on the cheek. They smiled at each other.

She was about to open the case, when Dermott indicated by pointing to his watch, that it was time to go. He wanted to be at the warehouse for six-thirty to load up so that he could be on the road again by lunchtime. Reluctantly, Irena replaced the case in her bag. He pulled on his heavy jacket, then helped her on with hers, a green, quarter-length coat more suited to spring and summer than to the biting chill of the Polish winter. She had been wearing that coat when they had first met, three months ago. She had been blue with cold, shivering and soaked through, standing alone just outside Pete's Place, the ramshackled bar where the drivers congregated between loads. Unaccompanied ladies were not admitted to Pete's Place.

He had missed his regular date, arriving late, delayed dropping off his container of motor-windings, and Irena had been the only girl remaining, left alone with no takers, her skinny, sodden appearance offputting to the men who usually preferred the tartish glamour of the more experienced bar girls.

Dermott had taken her inside for a drink, more out of pity than the prospect of a night of pleasure, which her obvious youthfulness and dowdiness told him would not be forthcoming. Indeed, that night he had slept upright in the driver's seat while she had taken the sleeping bag, falling off into a deep sleep the second she had lain down. In the morning, in her amateurish way, she had tried to make up for it, but Dermott had gently brushed off her feeble attempts to arouse him. She had not wanted to take his money, but he had forced it on her, together with some woollen socks which she still wore with her boots.

Their second time together had been awkward and frustrating for Dermott. She had led the way, pulled him into the sleeping compartment, helped him to undress, and his expectations had risen considerably. But it soon became clear that Irena knew very little about sex and the one-night stand and Dermott had been too shy to try and indicate exactly what he wanted. The language barrier and the darkened confinement had hindered Dermott's coy attempts at education and he had gone to sleep exhausted by his frustration. But he had to admit that the third time was much better, a big improvement, and this time, despite the liberal quantitites of drink he had consumed, had almost been spectacular.

She had obviously been learning her trade well in his absence and he detected a twinge of envy in himself. He liked her a lot, felt as if he had discovered her and felt protective towards her. Their conversations were limited to one or two words of each others' language interspersed with a wide variety of signs and facial expressions. If they could have talked together, he knew that he would have asked her about the other men she saw in between their twice-monthly meetings. And he knew he would be jealous of those men. In a way, he was glad they couldn't speak to one another: she couldn't tell him, he wouldn't have to know.

Irena pushed open her door and jumped out onto the tarmac, giving a cry of annoyance as she landed. Dermott climbed down and went round to her side to see her brushing water from her jeans and coat, as she stood in a pool of inky rain water. He took her hand but she pulled free and linked arms, resting her head against his shoulder. They crossed the park, heading for the main road, passing one of Irena's friends who had just descended from a Mercedes cab. They all said good morning to each other. The sun was just starting to push back the heavy blackness in the sky, changing its colour to several shades of purple in the east, while the wind continued to snap icy blasts across the slowly awakening city.

She snuggled in closer to him and buried the side of her face into the folds of his jacket as they turned the corner where Pete's Place stood and walked up Vilnius Street where Irena could catch a bus home. The roads were quiet and still, but, here and there, the headlights of cars and trucks could be seen weaving between the columns of workers' flats and office buildings.

They came to a halt next to a blue post box, just a few yards from the bus stop which was swathed in light. He pulled Irena to him and they kissed, once, twice, three times, quick, fond embraces. And then he wrapped his arms round her. She leant into him and kissed his face as they swayed together slightly, as if succumbing to the strength of the wind. He whispered goodbye in her ear and pushed her away. She looked sad, so he stroked her under the chin, and she smiled up at him. She half raised a hand to wave farewell, and, as she turned to go, Dermott casually dropped Mercer's letter into the blue posting box.

London, England

I

Tuert was talking but all eyes were on Mercer. 'They missed their morning call-up. The fall-back was three-twenty the same day. Nothing. Just like when Farmer went down. Cheltenham signalled no contact this morning. Nothing back at all.'

'Any other station report a contact? Harrogate, for example?' asked Binder.

'Harrogate?' said Fordyce.

'CIA station in North Yorkshire, sir,' said Tuert. 'No. Nothing from them,' Fordyce reddened.

'Even if they heard anything, they wouldn't tell us,' said Mercer.

Cameron interrupted angrily. 'Why did you say that? How do . . .?

'Gentlemen,' said Fordyce, the peacemaker. 'Enough.' Cameron folded his arms and sat back in his wooden chair. Mercer shifted about uncomfortably. His trousers were sticking to his thighs. And his favourite seat was no longer in the Director's office. He felt warm though the room was cooled by the whispering air-conditioning. His discomfort had nothing to do with the temperature, or the pine chair that creaked with newness whenever it was moved. 'This is a grave and serious matter and I will not tolerate any diversions.' He glared at Mercer, then Cameron. 'Carry on, Alfred.'

Tuert looked about him, surprised at being given the floor again. 'That's it, sir. The KGB have rolled up Doctor the same as they did Farmer.' Mercer was still the focal point of the assembly.

'Could it be that it is simply due to some malfunction in equipment, for example?' asked Fordyce. 'Or perhaps the radio operator is ill?'

'Not a chance,' said Mercer. 'Alf's right. The KGB have them. The network's blown'. He scratched his head slowly. 'There are contingency plans for mechanical failures, as it were. Emergency codes and contacts with Cheltenham. Even with Jones in the Embassy. But Farmer hasn't used any of them and they've been off the air for three weeks now. And I think it will be the same story for Doctor.'

Binder coughed. 'What have we had from Jones, then?' he asked. Mercer glanced across at him. Binder looked ill. He was pale and nervous, his voice mechanical as if he were just going through the motions. Binder's presence obviously indicated that he was to succeed Mercer as Head of Russia Section, but Mercer wondered why he hadn't so far put in an appearance in the Section to familiarise himself with its procedures. 'You've seen what he's got to say. Page two,' said Mercer. He flipped through his report. 'They've stitched him up.'

'Nothing more than that?' asked Cameron.

'If he can't get out and about with the KGB swarming everywhere, then he's not likely to produce much more,' replied Mercer.

'I suppose that's a further indication that Doctor and Farmer have been taken by the KGB? The increased surveillance of our Embassy Staff and the new restrictions on travel?' Fordyce waited for an answer.

Mercer supplied it. 'Yes. Plus Gromyko calling in the Ambassador for a dressing down yesterday.'

'Expulsions?' said Binder.

Mercer shrugged. 'Not unless the KGB can lay a trail back to us.'

'That shouldn't be too difficult with the methods they employ,' said Cameron. 'Anyway, since when do the Russians need proof before they start kicking Embassy staff back home?'

Fordyce held up his hands. 'Right, gentlemen. That will do. Alfred, as case-officer for Doctor, have you anything else to add?' Tuert said he had not and Fordyce asked him to leave. Tuert did so, the relief apparent on his face. As he closed the door behind him, Fordyce spoke again. 'Where do we go from here?' He looked around at his colleagues. They avoided his eyes. All except for the man on Fordyce's right. He actually smiled at the Director.

'I think this is where I come in,' announced Sidney Markfield. Nobody disagreed with him. Markfield struck a match and held it to his pipe. Cameron sniffed the air in disgust. Binder turned a paler shade of white. Mercer craved a cigarette. 'The bottom line, gentlemen,' he said between puffs, as he got the pipe going. 'We have a leak. A bloody big one.' He stopped puffing and surveyed the assembly. 'Right at the top.'

Markfield's Section dealt with the internal security of the Service. He was the master spy who spied on the spies. His staff, known as the auditors, were already in action inside Mercer's Section combing through files and folders, sifting and checking for any signs of treachery, accidental or purposeful, that could have led to the betrayal of Farmer. Networks did occasionally go down, for one reason or another. It was the task of the auditors to find out why, to try and uncover whether enemy action was responsible. If and when they found an answer, leaks were plugged, security tightened, and the occasional mole brought to the surface. Now, with Doctor going dead, Mercer reckoned that Markfield and his men would be in full cry. He shuddered at the prospect. His Section was already in turmoil, his staff in open revolt. There was a lot more to come.

Markfield completed his pipe ritual fully aware that he had everyone's attention, using the silence that had followed his introductory remarks to dramatic effect. 'We have a mole,' he said. '*Cedar* has forced him out into the open. It's a question of survival. The mole has got to get *Cedar* before *Cedar* can get him.'

'I agree,' said Cameron. 'We've had no serious breaches in security for some years now. The mole, I suspect, has been around for a long time, working his way through the Service, to a position of responsibility. The KGB had been hoping to use him when he had attained a high level appointment. But the advent of *Cedar* has meant that he has had to show himself earlier than anticipated in order to protect himself.'

'Then Markfield's job should be very simple, indeed,' said Mercer staring at Cameron. 'The mole is someone who has access to my Russian networks, together with knowledge of *Cedar's* existence. There can't be more than four or five people in the Service with that level of clearance.'

II

Mercer felt trapped, as if the walls of Century House were closing in on him. Wherever he went inside the building, eyes followed his every move. Some showed sympathy, others hostility and resentment, while a few smirked and laughed. It was a difficult thing to keep quiet within the tight-knit confines of the Service. But there was no willingness shown to help him. He was alone. Isolated. He was to blame. It was all his fault.

Mercer had been working feverishly for the past week to quell and calm his rebellious staff, and to cope with the extra workload Markfield's intrusion warranted. All communications from networks still in operation went directly to Mercer, who was virtually running the entire Section. But not very effectively. He couldn't concentrate with the queues of investigators peering over his shoulder, nor could he manage with his disgruntled staff who directed their anger and frustration at him.

And now Anderson, Dentist's case officer, had just confirmed what Mercer had heard earlier that morning, that Dentist had missed his weekly contact. A third network in trouble, he told himself. Three down. Four to go.

It didn't make any sense to Mercer. He tried to think it through. The Russian mole in the Service has surfaced to warn the KGB about *Cedar*. How had the mole heard of *Cedar*? Had he been present at Cameron's briefing? If he had, then he would know that it was Cameron alone who knew of *Cedar's* identity. No others had been involved in the contacts between Cameron and *Cedar*, certainly no one from any of Mercer's Russian networks. So what was the mole doing in betraying the networks to the KGB? The networks couldn't possibly provide the KGB with *Cedar's* identity. There would seem to be no point in betraying the networks.

Perhaps the mole had not been at the briefing but had heard of *Cedar* from one of those present. It would be understandable then, the mole assuming that *Cedar* had made contact through one of Mercer's networks. But Mercer couldn't see anybody who was at the briefing letting on about *Cedar* to anyone who didn't need to know. Careless talk, and all that. And there was still the problem that whoever the mole was, he still had to have access to all of the Russian networks. And as far as Mercer knew, there was only himself, Cameron and the Director with such access.

Mercer could not help the growing unease he felt which seemed to suggest that he was being set up. He could sense that the finger of suspicion was not just pointing at him, but was prodding him firmly in the chest. His resignation would have to be held in abeyance yet again: he could not leave now. That would look very suspicious. He was trapped.

MAY 1985
Krashnaya Kamni, Russia

I

The Caucasus Mountains, *Bolshoi Kavkas* in Russian, run from the Black Sea to the Caspian Sea. They separate the Russian Soviet Federal Socialist Republic from the Georgian and Azerbaydzhan Republics. The highest point in the range is Mount Elbruz, and during the spring and summer, when the air is clear and sharp, and the sky is a light, almost transparent blue, a climber standing on the summit, with his back to the three Russian Republics, can gaze down across a panoramic expanse which encompasses Turkey, Iraq and Iran.

Tucked away at the foot of the mountain range that slashes left to right across the isthmus between the two Seas, is the spa-town of Narzan, well known throughout the Soviet Union as the source of the Russian equivalent of Perrier water, and still a place of pilgrimage for elderly Russians with enough money, wishing to take the cure. High above Narzan, nestling in the glacial folds of the mountains, is the beautiful, secluded retreat of Krashnaya, Kamni, or Red Rocks.

Ordinary Russians wanting to travel beyond Narzan to the isolated hamlet would be met by armed guards of the Sluzbha, the Political Security Police, at several points on the rising track, who would demand to see not only identity cards but also the special passes that entitled the bearers to enter Krashnaya Kamni. Progress beyond the hamlet is not possible.

The Sluzbha guard the single-lane, black-topped road that climbs out of Krashnaya Kamni and terminates two hundred meters away in a tiny enclave of luxurious dachas surrounded by a high white wall. Only the

Sluzbha use the road. Visitors are ferried in by helicopter from the base at Stavropol airport 150 kilometers away down the mountain.

On Monday the sixth of May, the Premier of Russia was in residence. He used the dacha that had once been the summer home of his great friend and sponsor, Yuri Vladimirovich Andropov.

On the stroke of noon, the Sluzbha detachment inside the enclave were rudely roused from the torpor of their guard duty by the clacking stutter of a helicopter. It could be seen dead ahead, out over the plain, a dark spot on a canvas of blue, that grew with each beat of the rotors. The giant blades spun through the thin air, pushing the roar of the throbbing engines ahead of them, so that the din bounced and echoed around the mountain, shattering the peaceful tranquility of the beautiful haven. A highly polished black Zil saloon raced out of the compound to welcome the arrivals at the landing strip.

II

Viktor Chebrikov and Vitaly Fedorchuk did not bother to remove their hats as they stood waiting in the hallway while Major Nosenko performed the statutory protocol and went to announce their arrival.

Both men had an air of suppressed impatience about them, as if ready to explode into action at the drop of one of their hats, like generals eager to signal their troops forward in the decisive thrust. And generals they indeed were, though Fedorchuk, as Minister of the Interior, no longer used the title he had earned in the service of his country. Colonel General Chebrikov was head of the Komitet Gosudarstvennoi Bezopastnosti, the KGB, a position he had held for nearly three years.

As acolytes of former Premier Andropov, they had prepared the way for his chosen successor and had seen him installed in power following the year-long interregnum of the feeble Chernenko. Now they waited on their master, barely two months in office, to confront him once again with the crisis that could undo all their schemes and plans for the future security of Mother Russia.

Major Nosenko strode along the short corridor that led to the Premier's inner sanctum. Fedorchuk took off his hat, his eyes alert, monitoring the Major's return. 'The Comrade Premier will join you in a moment,' he said formally, before resuming his station.

Fedorchuk slapped his hat against his thigh and swung round to face Chebrikov. An uncompromising look of commitment and agreement passed between them. They were both determined to have their way. Chebrikov began to pace. Major Nosenko observed his two superiors as he pretended to read, noting the nervous tension that infected them. Fedorchuk was now fretfully twisting the brim of his hat.

'Viktor. Vitaly,' said the Premier, as he came along the corridor. He held out his hands and embraced both men, his face unsmiling. 'We will walk.' He led the way outside.

Chebrikov and Fedorchuk fell in behind, one on either side. A glimmer of a smile came to the Premier's lips. He could see the worry in their faces. Not a word was spoken as the small procession made its way along the broad avenue between the villas towards the clearing and the man-made lake. Six Sluzbha guardians followed at a respectful distance.

Chebrikov coughed, prepared to speak, as they stopped beneath a tall conifer. The Premier held up his hand. 'I understand,' he said. His eyes looked down into the crystal clear water of the lake. 'Suslov's creation,' he said. 'It is fed by an underwater stream. He kept it well stocked. But I have little time to enjoy the relaxation of a day's fishing.' He sighed deeply. 'None of us has the time. We cannot afford it. Am I right, Vitaly?'

'Yes, Comrade Premier,' said Fedorchuk. 'The . . .'

'I know you both very well,' interrupted the Premier. 'I know what you want.' He walked on a way and spoke over his shoulder. 'You have found out nothing. You have no name for me.' He stopped and turned. 'And now you want my sanction. You will not leave without it?' Chebrikov nodded. Fedorchuk stood firmly in front of his chief.

'We must act now,' said Fedorchuk stiffly.

'Indeed we must,' said the Premier. 'We have no other option. Golden Fleece is our only hope.' He smiled at his two aides. 'That is what you wanted to hear, was it not? And that is what I am saying.'

'Everything is ready,' said Fedorchuk. 'Viktor has seen to that.'

'I should think so,' replied the Premier. 'The operation is Andropov's. Formulated a decade ago. You both have had a month to prepare it for implementation according to the guide-lines.'

'Do you want to see it, Comrade?' asked Chebrikov.

'Tell me who is involved.'

'The ground-man will be Todor Zarev,' said Chebrikov as if reading from a list. 'Born in . . .'

'I know of Todor. The Team Leader, Viktor.'

'Yes, Comrade. Doctor Pavel Yosipovich Pastukhov.'

'He was top of the list of the four candidates selected,' interposed Fedorchuk.

'I remember,' said the Premier. 'An excellent choice.' He considered for a moment. 'The others I do not need to know about. Except that they will not be Russians.'

'True, Comrade Premier. Foreign mercenaries,' said Chebrikov. 'As stated in the original operational analysis.'

'Yes,' said the Premier, as if he had the original document in front of him now. 'Todor will do the cleaning up as well?' Chebrikov nodded. 'That is very important. The British are nobody's fool. They will know it was us. But if there's no one left after the operation for them to use, to parade in front of the world's press, then they will say and do nothing.'

'That is the way it has been planned,' said Fedorchuk.

III

The red and white Yak-40 was an hour's flying time away from Tushino, the KGB's private airfield on the outskirts of Moscow. Fedorchuk was asleep, slumped against the window, his breathing heavy and stentorian, as a result of the vodka he had rapidly consumed in celebration as soon as he had boarded the flight. Chebrikov sat behind him, wide awake, sipping a glass of beer. He had not felt like celebrating. Fedorchuk's work was over. His own was just beginning: Golden Fleece.

It was their only option. Failure? He shuddered at the thought. There could be no question of failure. *Cedar* had to be unmasked.

The British networks he had rounded up did not even know of *Cedar's* existence let alone his identity. Of this he was convinced. The mole inside MI6 had just now reported through Guk that the identity of *Cedar* was known by only one man in London. But he had had to check that out, just in case one of the networks had been involved with the recruitment of *Cedar*.

It was a great pity that the mole in the Service had had to surface prematurely, before his promotion to the highest grade. His value to the KGB would have been immense. But he had been forced into revealing himself as a matter of survival when *Cedar* arrived. The mole hunters would be after him now. His days were numbered. Markfield would have him shortly.

IV

Major Nosenko uncorked the bottle of chilled Chornye Glaza and poured a glass for the Premier. He could almost taste the delicate, light flavour of the wine which to him readily captured the very spirit of the southern part of the country. But he knew he would have to be content with a couple of bottles of Zhigulyovshoye beer and some black bread and cheese. The Premier would not invite him to his table tonight: he was too deep in thought.

The Premier reached across the table and picked up a silver salver. As Nosenko withdrew, he absentmindedly spooned the caviar and fish-in-aspic onto his plate. Next he piled on some pickles and cucumbers, and several bright Bulgarian tomatoes, and began to eat. Nosenko returned a few minutes later with a plate of shashlyks of grey mullet, fresh from the Caspian Sea. But the Premier ignored them, as he did his wine. Nosenko shrugged and left his master to himself.

Cedar, he thought. The name haunted him. A nightmare. The previous night he had dreamt of a giant, black tree waving its spiky, pointed branches at him, taunting him, mocking him. A huge pendulum had pushed it to one side and began to count off the days, the months as if they were fractions of seconds. Time. *Cedar*. His two greatest enemies. They laughed at him.

Golden Fleece was his only practical option. It had been forced on him, was very risky. But not half as dangerous as trying to neutralise *Cedar* by arresting the Politburo. Such a confrontation, reviving memories of Stalin's purges, would only result in his own demise. He was not strong enough for such a showdown.

He needed time. With the help of Chebrikov and Fedorchuk, he was moving his people into position, working to Andropov's blue-print, his timetable. Geldar Aliyev had been the latest appointment: his experience as KGB chief of Azerbaydzhan would soon be brought to bear against the corrupt monsters and black-market thieves that had thrived under Brezhnev.

How could he, the leader of the Russian people, demand loyalty from his fellow citizens to the State when its bureaucrats and officials so openly flaunted their criminality? How could he curb the dissidents, when all they had to do was point the finger at those vagabonds and ask if this was the State they were expected to follow and admire?

The problem of dissent and dissatisfaction would not simply disappear by the application of force, or with the arrest and incarceration of the protesters. The Russian knout would not solve the difficulties. Compromises had to be reached with those who were disillusioned and alienated; solutions found and implemented, slowly and gradually. He needed time. Corruption had to be weeded out and eliminated. More money had to be injected into industry, agriculture, education and the medical services. The people had to have something to look forward to, something to look up to. He needed money.

Andropov, he thought, had been correct. The financing of the reform programmes could only come from the military budget – from the ever-growing, all-consuming nuclear arms development costs. The hawks and hardliners of the Politburo and the National Defence Council had been shoved out into the wings by their insistence on a military solution to Afghanistan. Now their noses were bloodied. They were silent men now, though still watching and waiting for the right opportunity for a come-back. He needed time. Time to reach an accommodation with the West. Time to put a halt to the spiralling arms race. Russia could no longer afford to take part in the race. She was in danger of collapsing under the financial burden.

The leitmotiv of his foreign policy, like Andropov's was the 'struggle for peace'. But his efforts to date had not met with any success in the West. They were suspicious of him and becoming more belligerent and bellicose in response to his peace-feelers. He knew that a great deal of this renewed aggressiveness stemmed from *Cedar's* treachery. The West thought they had all the cards.

A new round of SALT talks were due in the summer. He was determined to make one final push for an accommodation. But *Cedar* would betray his position. The Americans would be negotiating from strength, trying to push him into a corner, weaken him, force an agreement that benefitted the West at the expense of Mother Russia. But he could never do that. The Great Patriotic War was still fresh in the minds of the Russian people. They might moan and groan about their standard of living, but let them give up one missile, one tiny portion of the country's defence under pressure, and the people would have him out.

He would not, could not, negotiate under duress. The Americans would press him at the SALT talks, but there would be no compromise, no accommodation. And Russia would then be labelled as the war-monger, as the one not willing to stop the arms spiral. And the West would have all the justification necessary for its recent missile deployments. Then the Kremlin hawks would come striding in from their hide-outs, demanding the finance for further weapons to keep apace of the West. The arms spiral would continue. The reform programmes would be starved of money, the corruption and dissent would continue and Mother Russia would once again be on the road to self-destruction.

The Premier stood up suddenly from the table, his meal only half-finished. He had to have *Cedar*. And quickly. The talks in Geneva were due to begin in July.

London, England

I

It was Samuel Pepys, the noted diarist, who, as Secretary for War under Charles II, was responsible for the establishment of Greenwich as a naval base. For it is at Greenwich that the two main avenues from the south of the City, the river Thames and the road from Dover, come together. Greenwich also occupies the last of the high ground along the embankment from where the City could be defended, and the land, in the Crown's possession since the Middle Ages, was given over to Pepys and his band of architects to build the last redoubt.

On his left, Mercer noted the mooring points of the Cutty Sark and Sir Francis Chichester's Gypsy Moth, while to his right, the National Maritime Museum and the Royal Greenwich Observatory, built thirteen and a half degrees off true north, were signposted in a confusing array of arrows. He brought his car to a halt at the traffic lights. His fingers tapped out the beat of *Monday, Monday* on the steering wheel. He headed towards Woolwich, passing under the flyover, following the main road, until he turned right into the housing estate of pebble-dashed concrete boxes. There was a smell of burnt sugar in the air.

The streets were littered with derelict cars and wind-blown paper scraps, the tumbleweed of urban renewal. A surburban train roared past, an hourly escape route for the tenants of the sprawl. The estate petered out at the top of the hill where it ran into several streets of Edwardian houses suffering from terminal neglect. Mercer parked his car on the boundary between the old and the newly-old and made for the last stand of concrete hutches.

He took the dusty steps to the second floor where he rang the bell of number thirty-five. Dermott Whelan opened the door almost immediately. 'Just hang on there,' he said before retreating into the hallway. He returned a few seconds later, his arms crab-like above his head as he struggled into a thin jacket. 'The wife's in,' he said. 'And me ma's in bed.' He straightened out his jacket and pulled the door to behind him. Mercer stood to one side to let him pass.

Whelan led the way down to ground level and Mercer caught up to him as he turned to go down the hill. 'She's fallen out with her mate again,' explained Whelan, jerking his head backwards in the direction of the flat. 'Wouldn't go to Bingo. Always the same when you want them to go out.' He dug his hands into his trouser pockets and shrugged his shoulders, the gesture betraying his lack of comprehension of the female mind.

'Where are we going?' asked Mercer.

'To the pub.' He looked across at Mercer and received a nod of approval. 'Won't be too busy, yet.'

They crossed the main road and entered another sector of the sprawl, both men deftly swerving around the land mines of dog shit which seemed to cover most of the pavement. But there were no dogs on the streets, just small groups of young boys engaged in various forms of mischief to the accompaniment of blaring stereos.

'I didn't know your mother lived with you,' said Mercer, by the way of conversation.

'Got fed up with Liverpool. She moved in while I was away.' Whelan shrugged again. 'I don't think she likes it, though. Too noisy.'

They were nearing the Woolwich Road and the pattern of sound was changing, the background of electronic noise giving way to that of the rumbling traffic. 'The traffic you mean?' asked Mercer.

'No. Them next-door in thirty-seven. The Murtaghs. Bloody nutcases,' he said in disgust. 'Always fighting, y'know.'

'Really,' said Mercer.

'He drinks. She plays Bingo with the missus. When they get together they fight.'

'Your wife and Mrs, er, Murtagh' said Mercer with a frown, not quite following Whelan's explanation.

'No. Him and her.'

'I see. And it disturbs your mother.'

'The walls are paper-thin, see.' They turned into the Woolwich Road. 'Not far to go. Just down there by the wall.' Mercer couldn't see the wall but he did not mention the fact.

'Anyway,' continued Whelan. 'She's only tiny.' He held out a hand, palm parallel to the ground, at chest height. 'And he's bigger than me.' He raised the hand above his head. 'Big red nose, big red face, just like a smacked arse. But she don't half give it to him.' He smiled to himself. 'Belted him over the head with a frying-pan yesterday.'

'She must have quite a reach on her,' said Mercer, mentally calculating the difference in heights between 'him and her'.

'He was in bed at the time. You could hear the bang in our living-room. Woke me ma up.'

'It would do.'

'I miss most of their shenanigans when I'm away.'

'How was your trip?' asked Mercer hurriedly, to change the subject.

'Nowt special. Same as usual.'

'No trouble at the borders?' Mercer watched his companion out of the corner of his eye. Whelan's face was open and honest. If there had been a problem Mercer would see it there, in the eyes and the mouth. But Whelan continued as before.

'No. All you've got to watch is your time. As you cross into East Germany they give you a time card. You hand that in at the German-Polish border and providing you've crossed Germany in the given time, everything's OK.'

'No searches?'

'Just a quick once over.' He glanced at Mercer.

'Personal ones, eh?'

He nodded his head. 'No. Nothing like that.' The two men shook their heads in unison. 'Here we are,' said Whelan. Mercer saw the wall before he saw the pub.

They went into the bar where two men were playing darts. 'It's Dermott,' said the man tugging the darts from the board. 'You're back.'

'Looks like it, doesn't it?' said Whelan, as he approached the counter. 'Alright, Geoff?'

The barman grinned. 'Fine, Dermott. You're looking well.'

'I know. I know. All this fresh air. Give us a pint.' He turned to Mercer. 'What y'having?'

'Gin and tonic. Here. Let me get them,' said Mercer, coming to stand next to Whelan. 'Ice in the gin please.' Mercer pulled out his wallet. Geoff pulled Dermott's pint.

Whelan pressed in close to Mercer. 'Watch them two at the dartboard.' Mercer looked over at them. They smiled at him. 'Don't let them inveigle you into buying them a drink.' He pointed at Mercer's wallet. 'They know you've got money.'

'Right,' said Mercer.

'They won't work, them two,' added Whelan by way of an explanation. 'Always on the bum. Got round shoulders from pushing open pub doors. Idle buggers.' Mercer said he understood. Whelan carried his beer over to a table near the dart board. Mercer watched him with his two cronies as he waited for his drink. Whelan was talking in a low voice, and an occasional glance was directed towards Mercer, the new face, the topic of conversation. He paid for the drinks and walked over to join them.

Whelan knocked back half of his drink in one gulp. 'Right,' he said, wiping the froth from his mouth with the back of his hand. 'We'll take these two on.'

'Okay,' said Mercer.

'Tommy,' said the fat one, and held out his hand to Mercer.

'Billy,' said the one who had announced Whelan's arrival.

'John,' lied Mercer, and shook their hands.

Mercer and Whelan lost the first game, but narrowly won the second. As Tommy wiped the board clean for the third game, Mercer excused himself and went to the toilet. He was certain now that he hadn't been followed: no one had entered the bar room since his and Whelan's entrance.

The toilet smelt of carbolic and urine, strong and pungent, causing Mercer to wrinkle his nose in protest. He stood in the centre stall, his feet well back from the trough which was partially flooded because of a crop of cigarette ends protruding from the single drain. 'Vote communist or we're fucked' said the graffitti directly in front of his eyes. He heard the door creak open and Whelan came to join him.

Mercer zipped up his fly and took out an envelope from his inside pocket. He balanced it on the porcelain divider between the two stalls next to Whelan's shoulder. Whelan half-turned to look and splashed urine over his shoes. 'Shit,' he said. Then, 'Piss', and laughed. When he had finished he scooped up the envelope and replaced it with another. Both men tucked them away in their pockets. 'No problems. Picked it up at Pete's Place.'

Mercer knew all about the truckers' rendezvous. He had paid a visit once while working in Warsaw. Once had been enough. 'Thanks,' said Mercer. He rinsed his hands. There was no towel, though.

II

Mercer got home after midnight. He had had to drive slowly and carefully because of the half a dozen gins he had consumed. He had not intended staying so late at the pub, but as the evening progressed, he found he was enjoying himself. They had been joined by another friend of Whelan's, Rob Standish, who like Whelan, was a long-distance lorry driver. Both had kept the company well entertained with their stories of trips on the continent, especially into the communist bloc countries, where their time schedules were very often interrupted by diversions with the local girls.

While standing in the untidy kitchen waiting for the kettle to boil he noticed the book lying on the table under the sugar bowl and picked it up. He brushed the few grains of sugar from the cover and tried to think of a place to put it so he would not forget to take it with him in the morning.

Jan Orleszewski would be expecting it. He put it back on the kitchen table, promising himself to eat some breakfast in the morning. He placed the packet of Corn Flakes on top of it.

Steam began to fill the room. He brewed a cup of black coffee and took it through into the living room, drew the curtains and turned on the table lamps before sitting down on the sofa. He drank slowly, savouring the moment rather than the plastic taste of the coffee, like a man who knew the answer to the $64,000 question, and was waiting for the question to be asked. He placed his empty cup on the floor and took out Whelan's envelope. He leant across the low table and picked up the ABC of airline schedules, rested it on his knee, and opened the envelope.

It contained a single sheet of typed paper on which there were thirteen names. Mercer scanned the list. The names belonged to the thirteen members of the Soviet

Politburo. The first seven had a zero next to them and he assumed that this meant they had not left Russia during the crucial time period. The remaining six names were followed by a series of dates and destinations. He concentrated on these. He opened the ABC at the first paper marker which gave BA flights to Paris at the time of Cameron's trip there. None of the six Politburo members were anywhere in the region according to the list.

He checked the names against Cameron's Berlin trip; nothing. It was just the same for the other two European journeys Cameron had made. He put the ABC on the table and began a more detailed search, to see whether Cameron, unbeknown to London, could have made an onward journey to meet with one of the names.

After an hour, his eyes tired from reading the small print, he concluded that Cameron had been lying. He could not have met with the member of the Politburo at the times he had said he had. Mercer realised that his assumption rested upon the accuracy of the list from the Polish network: but they had always been right before. They had never let him down: 'Politburo watching' was one of the games they played in earnest since the appearance of a member of the Politburo in one of the eastern bloc countries, usually spelt trouble somewhere along the line.

Mercer sat back in the sofa and closed his eyes. Cameron was lying. Why? What possible reasons could he have? Had he made contact with a lesser Soviet official and was trying to boost his own prestige by claiming that it was a contact inside the Politburo? Mercer didn't think so: the level and standard of intelligence would quickly expose that lie. Then why?

He got to his feet and stretched. He was too tired to think clearly. He would sleep on it, then check it all again in the morning when his mind would be a lot clearer. He pulled off his tie as he walked through the bedroom. The floor was littered with yesterday's clothing and he stooped to gather it all together and

bundled it into a ball which he threw in a wicker w.
basket. He straightened out the duvet and boxed the
pillows into shape.

As he was taking off his socks and shoes, he could not
help wondering whether the mole had trodden the same
path as he had to check out Cameron's claim. And if he
had, what conclusions he and the KGB had come to.

Moscow, Russia

I

The intercom buzzed. Pavel flicked the switch. 'Yes?' he said.

A tinny voice replied. 'Madame Svanidze has just called to cancel.'

'Thank you, Sonya. Did she make another appointment?'

'For next Friday. Same time.'

'Who's next?'

'Madame Budenny is the last.'

'That's good,' said Pavel. He released the switch and rubbed his hands together. He picked up his pen and looked down at the case-notes. After a moment's hesitation, he wrote just one word, 'overreacting', and underlined it. He turned the notes face down on the desk blotter and sat back in his chair to await the reappearance of the formidable Madame Budenny.

To his left a floral sight-screen stood angled to the wall. From behind it came the noise of a big woman trying to struggle into a dress that cried out for a slimmer body. Nadya Alliluyeva Budenny huffed and puffed as she fought to insert her rolls of fat into the Paris creation.

Pavel closed his eyes and mentally relaxed. It had been a hard day. He listened to the noises that emanated from behind the screen and he was aware that his face hardened. He heard the screen being pushed aside. He sat up straight and gave a smile, as automatic and as phoney as a politician's handshake, which crinkled his features and lightened his eyes.

The huge woman, red of face, waddled up to his desk. She lowered herself into the chair and placed her hands on the desk as if to give herself additional support, not wanting to entirely trust the fragile seat. Her eyes, black and bloodshot, were hooded under folds of flesh, and her voice, when she spoke, was child-like and whimpering.

'What is it, Doctor?' she asked, and her painted face assumed the expression of one prepared for the worst, a prisoner awaiting a sentence of death.

Pavel swallowed. He allowed himself a moment to co-ordinate his voice and expression so that he could cope with the apparent gravity of the women's illness.

'I'm not sure, Nadya Alliluyeva.' He heard the woman's short intake of breath. One hand was raised to the gigantic bosom. The other gripped the edge of the desk. 'We will need to do some tests.'

The woman pushed herself back in her seat and her head lolled to one side. Pavel could see the conflicting emotions of joy and fear dance across her flaccid face. He could imagine her with her friends, all cast in the same mould, boasting that the good Doctor Pavel had at last detected some sign of the illness that had plagued her for so long: then the voice would falter, the hand would go to the forehead, and her friends would rush about solicitously for a chair, a glass of water and the smelling salts. When you were the wife of the Chairman of Party Organs, you had friends who did that. It was a dangerous precedent, thought Pavel. If Madame Budenny had something wrong with her, then Madame Antonov must surely be ill, too. Her husband was of the same rank as Budenny. Then there would be Madame Karamzin and all the others in pecking order who would all demand that Pavel find something wrong with them. No one could, or would, be left out. The epidemic would spread rapidly.

'We will do the tests tomorrow,' said Pavel, his voice grave. Madame Budenny closed her eyes and slowly nodded her head. Pavel bit his tongue. That had been a mistake, he thought. He should have made it sometime next week. Tomorrow suggested an urgency which did not exist and which would be exploited by this overweight dragon. Madame Antonov, he knew, would be at his surgery first thing in the morning when she heard.

115

'If you see Sonya on your way out, she will arrange a time,' added Pavel.

Using the arms of the chair as support, Madame Budenny heaved her bulk out of the seat with great effort, the strain twisting her mouth into a grimace. She tottered to her feet and looked down at Pavel.

'Thank you,' she whispered and turned away, her head sagging forward, her walk unsteady and erratic. She had not the strength to close the door behind herself. Pavel watched her disappearing figure in a state of mild apprehension, knowing that this case of chronic indigestion was going to cause him quite a few headaches in the next week or so, particularly as he was in close proximity to many of his patients.

II

Pavel lived in the Arbat district of Moscow, on the ground floor of a very select tower block, which also housed a Marshal and two Generals of the Red Army, three members of the Central Committee, and one member of the Politburo. The block next door accommodated the families of equally well-known high-ranking nomenclatura, including Vasili Budenny and his hypochondriac wife.

He did not mind living on the ground floor, as this meant he had access to part of the basement where he had installed, over the years, a small sauna and multi-gym. His surgery was the apartment directly above his own and the State had allowed him to build a staircase through to the surgery from his ground floor living quarters. It was the least the State could do for the man who prescribed for the wives and children of the vlasti and nomenclatura.

Every evening after surgery his routine was the same: an hour's workout in the gym followed by half an hour in the heat of the sauna. He was fit and well, he did not smoke and only drank in moderation. His only wish was that his patients would do the same. In a way, he did not blame them. Their husbands had little or no time for them, being tied to the never-ending rounds of committees, debates and functions. They were the wives of the elite and privileged in a society where such things did not officially exist. They shopped in the special sectors of the GUM department stores, and in the Beriozka shops, which provided all the luxuries of the decadent West. Their homes were crammed with all the electrical and electronic gadgetry that Japan and America could muster. They spent their winters away from the ice-bound streets of Moscow, down in their dachas on the Black Sea. They were spoiled and pampered, as were their children. But most of all, they were bored. They ate too much and became frustrated when their figures could not match those of the actresses and ballerinas their husbands periodically squired; or when their imported gowns and dresses resisted the invasion of their bodies; or when Pavel, after many, many examinations could find nothing wrong with them that a sensible diet and moderate exercise would not cure. As for their children, there was a bitter harvest to be reaped when they came of age. He had seen it all while he was in training: the drug and alcohol abuse, petty criminality, the disenchantment and boredom with privilege that led to the psychiatric wards.

One day, he kept telling himself, it would be interesting to break from the role of pill-pusher and amateur psychologist and concentrate on real medicine among real people that truly needed help and support. One day.

III

He went upstairs, his body wrapped in a terry bathrobe, still shivering from his cold shower. He stopped off in the kitchen to pour himself a glass of Wyborowa, his favourite Polish vodka, then carried on into the bedroom. He turned on the television and started to dress. The face of Gely Dzerzhinsky, fronting the nightly news programme, Vremya, blinked onto the screen. He watched it for a few minutes, then turned down the sound.

From the bedside table he picked up some hand-written notes and began to read. As a member of the Moscow Hippodrome Racing Committee, the equivalent of the British Jockey Club, he was preparing for the start of another flat racing season. He would be very busy for the next week or two putting the final touches to the opening programme. He was looking forward to it with great excitement. The thoroughbred gave him his only release from the doctor's chair.

His interest had first been aroused as a youth by his mother, who had told him of his father's part in the storming of the Winter Palace during the Revolution. Later, Pavel's father had led his men on a foraging expedition for food, and had arrived at the Imperial Racing Club in St Petersburg. Several thoroughbreds were stabled there, amongst them Aboyeur, winner of the 1913 Epsom Derby, the Suffragette Derby.

Aboyeur was slaughtered along with the rest, and Pavel's mother said his father's troop had eaten the unfortunate animal. Pavel had been both amazed and incredulous at his father's escapade until he had looked up the story of Aboyeur in a racing journal. From that time on he had been hooked on horses.

The telephone rang as he entered the living room. He was expecting a call from the Committee's Secretary. 'Hullo,' he said as he picked up the receiver.

'Pavel Yosipovich Pastukhov?' asked a man's voice.

Pavel frowned. He did not recognise the voice. 'Speaking,' he said slowly, momentarily confused.

'The Don has broken its banks,' said the voice.

'Pardon. Who is this? What did you say?' He was nonplussed now.

'The Don has broken its banks. Do you understand, Comrade Doctor?'

'I'm sorry, but . . .' Realisation suddenly struck Pavel. 'My apologies, Comrade.' It had come so unexpectedly. He cursed himself. That was the way they said it would come. 'The harvest will be ruined,' he said.

'The people must build dykes,' came the reply.

'They must build them with their hands.' Pavel let out a sigh of relief.

'Eight o'clock. The Metro near the Lenin Museum. The Marx Prospekt entrance.' The line went dead.

Pavel sat down and breathed deeply.

Yurlovo, Russia

I

It was only when the black Zil saloon drove onto the Volokolamskoye Highway that Pavel had an idea of where he was going. He had been met at the Metro entrance by a tall elegant man, who, with a smile playing around the corners of his mouth had repeated the *parole* that Pavel and his mysterious caller had enunciated earlier that evening. They had descended into the catacombs of the Metro and travelled aimlessly from station to station, from line to line, for two hours, eventually emerging at the Nikitsky Gates where the Zil had been waiting. Pavel went on alone, the silent driver his only company.

They passed through the village of Yurlovo and turned off the road onto a single-lane track where a red and white barrier blocked their progress. Two armed men, khaki-clad, approached the vehicle and examined the passes the bored driver was waving from his window. It only took a second or two for the guards to realise the significance of their visitors and the barrier was raised very swiftly. Within minutes, Pavel was deposited at the main gates of the the Foreign Intelligence School. The Zil roared off, heading back the way it had come.

In the two years that Pavel had spent at the School after graduating from Medical College, he had never seen it like this before. In the dark he could just make out the tall wooden fence that surrounded the compound, but he could not see into the inky void, because of the barbed wire that topped it. The sentry boxes were empty, and the blazing lights that normally burnt day and night had been turned off. The School looked deserted.

He heard the whine of a small electric motor. 'Step forward,' ordered a tinny voice. Pavel walked up to the gate and was suddenly blinded by a beam of light. 'Stand still. Face the camera.' He blinked into the light, and then he saw it, a red dot in the centre of the gate. Someone made a final adjustment, and the camera pointed directly at his face. 'Through the sentry box on the left. If you please, Comrade Doctor,' said the disembodied voice.

II

'You will remember from the time you spent here that you were part of an élite,' said Viktor Chebrikov. 'A secret and trusted élite, kept apart from all the others. There were six of you. Yes?'

'Yes,' said Pavel.

'Comrade Andropov's secret army.' He smiled. 'Our former Chairman tried to plan for all contingencies. He was a wise man.'

Pavel closed his eyes for a moment. He was tired and he longed to stretch out on the bed upon which he sat. A picture of Andropov appeared before him: the bright hazel eyes ringed by rimless spectacles, the hair, thick and white, swept back from the forehead, his face ashen, etched in deep fatigue. He had been Pavel's saviour and benefactor.

'You have read the Premier's letter?' Chebrikov was speaking again. Pavel opened his eyes. 'You understand the enormity of our, er, problem?'

'I do,' replied Pavel.

Chebrikov held out his hand. Pavel gave him the letter. 'You can sleep now. Do you remember Lev Guryanov? The one you all used to call Babushka . . .' Pavel said yes. 'Good. He will be your instructor throughout your stay here. Besides a handful of guards, you two will be the only people at the school. I must return to Moscow.' He stood up and shook Pavel by the hand. 'You will work hard and be ready to go in two weeks. Good-bye, Pavel Yosipovich.'

Pavel slumped down on the bed. He did not bother to

undress. He would only have time for an hour or two's rest. Babushka began every day at the crack of dawn.

He dozed fitfully until Lev Guryanov came for him. Images of his days at the School paraded themselves before him. Two hard years without a break. There had been no time for fun, for laughter. And then he saw his father. At first he was like the photograph that Pavel kept in his study, brown and white, stiff and stern, obviously proud of his captain's uniform. That picture faded and dissolved: now his father was smiling, laughing his booming laugh. Summer in Gorky Park. Pavel was shrieking with pleasure as the Big Dipper hurtled them through twists and turns. A small boy clinging to the bulk of his father.

It was Pavel's favourite memory, the only one that really stood out. For some reason Pavel's father had fallen foul of one of Stalin's minions and had died in the Lubyanka. In those days Pavel's lot should have been that of his father, but for the intervention of Yuri Andropov, then an up and coming KGB officer. He had been political commissar alongside Pavel's father at the siege of Leningrad during the Great Patriotic War. He had saved Pavel and his mother. Pavel had had only one answer when Andropov personally approached him just before graduation. He owed the man his life.

III

Pavel had the file in front of him. Guryanov was speaking as he read, picking out the salient points. 'Zarev, Todor. Fifty-six. Native of Plevin in northern Bulgaria. Both parents members of Commintern. Both died during the fascist invasion. Taken to the Stara Mountains by an uncle, and began killing Germans when he was twelve. In 1945 he became a member of the Darjavna Sigurnost, Bulgaria's KGB, campaigning against fascist remnants in the south. In '47, he was sent to

Moscow for training at the First Chief Directorate's School at Kuchino, and later attached to the Executive Action Department.'

Pavel allowed himself a ghost of a smile at the linguistic gymnastics the KGB employed to cover their activities. Todor Zarev was a professional assassin.

Guryanov continued. 'He was the first Bulgarian to receive a commission in the Committee for State Security and he currently holds the rank of Colonel.' Pavel could see why. A long list of Zarev's accomplishments followed the biography in the file. 'He will be your ground man. Get to know him. Like a lover. He knows you. And don't be put off by his age.'

'Don't worry,' said Pavel. 'I won't be.'

London, England

I

'Good night, Mr Swainson.'

'Good night, Judith.' He checked his watch from habit as Judith smiled and closed the door. He was surprised when he saw that it was five-thirty. Where had the day gone? he asked himself as he got to his feet. And where had Simpson got to? Then he remembered the late appointment at the Kingston branch. It was no use, he would have to have more staff. Perhaps even another office.

He packed his briefcase: sandwich box, a wad of advertising leaflets for final approval, and two contracts for signature. He snapped the case shut and collected his hat and rolled umbrella from the back of the door, before returning to his desk to glance at his diary. Mr Saleem Sayed, nine-thirty, then nothing until after lunch. He did not have as much contact with the clients as he used to, the junior partners looked after that now, but he liked to keep his hand in with the occasional client, providing it didn't take him too far from the office. Knightsbridge. A short lease for Mr Sayed.

He went through into the outer office and took down the booklet marked Knightsbridge and squeezed it into his case. The room was silent, the typewriters hooded and still, the clatter of machines and voices in abeyance until tomorrow morning. He noticed that the waste-paper bins had not been emptied, and that Judith's was overflowing onto the floor. He made a mental note to speak to the cleaning contractor in the morning: he insisted that the bins be emptied before six every day, and that both offices should be cleaned and locked by seven.

There was no sign of the cleaners in the corridor as he waited for the lift. They were obviously slacking. He was not going to stand for that. He went down to the ground floor and turned left along the Gloucester Road, heading for the tube station.

The evening was cool and pleasant and he did not hurry, threading his way along the crowded pavement with the ease and assurance of a man at peace with the world. Those pedestrians who noticed him saw a man in his middle fifties, almost six feet tall, greying at the temples beneath his bowler hat, swinging both his briefcase and umbrella in a very casual manner. His back was straight, his whole bearing had a military air, and the keen observer would have spotted the Royal Artillery tie and assumed he had once been an officer.

He took the Circle line to Victoria and crossed over to the Southern Region for the train to Purley. He was in time for the ten past six train which was running late. He would have to wait for his wife to collect him at the other end as he usually caught the thirty-eight minutes past which arrived at seven o'clock.

His usual carriage, the third one behind the engine, was full, so he moved one down and even then only just managed to get a seat, emerging the victor over a young lady, loaded down with shopping, by a whisper. He hid behind his copy of *The Times*, not looking up until the train rolled into East Croydon, eight minutes late by his reckoning.

He did not have long to wait for his wife who drove up sedately in his Volvo. They exchanged pleasantries about each other's day on the short drive to Purley Rise where she parked the car in the driveway of number eight.

Inside, he handed over his lunch box before depositing his case in the study. He ate alone, a ham and cheese salad with brown bread, then joined his wife in the day room for a glass wine. They had no children, so their evening chats were given over to local gossip and the workings of the many committees his wife sat on. About eight-thirty, Swainson left his wife and adjourned to the study to 'sort out a spot of paperwork.'

The work was not urgent and could have been done during office hours, but he always brought something home with him every evening to give him the excuse to leave her. In the early days of Swainson Estates, while he had been building up the business, their time together had been very limited. And now that he was a success, he found he had nothing in common with his wife. He found her company tedious, and an hour of it was all he could bear. He could have retired tomorrow: the junior partners could run the business without him, and he had plenty of money invested to provide for him in retirement. But that would have meant spending more time with Anne. The evenings and week-ends were bad enough; the week-days would be disastrous.

He began to skim through the Knightsbridge folder for a suitable property for Mr Sayed. Thank goodness for the Arabs, he told himself. It was not until the late sixties that Swainson Estates had really established itself in London and the Home Counties. And it was thanks to the influx of the Middle Eastern gentlemen. Swainson has seen the attraction of London both as an investment opportunity and as a watering-hole to the Arabs, and he had been one of the first estate agents to offer his services. Now he had five branch offices, and he employed forty staff. He was also part of the referral system operated between the top ten agencies in and around London, and he had contacts nationwide, even extending into Europe and America.

He was proud of his success but had not let it go to his head. He and his wife led simple, almost frugal, lives, their only luxury being the twice yearly trip to the Bahamas where they had a small estate. He did not smoke and only drank wine. His one fault, a vanity really, was the Royal Artillery tie and the impression he liked to cultivate of having been an officer. He had seen military service in West Germany, but that had been in the Pay Corps when he had been called up for National Service, and he had only reached the rank of corporal.

But he never thought of those days: even his wife did not know of his time spent in Germany.

'Robert,' said his wife, peering around the study door. He looked up from his reading. 'There's a gentleman to see you. A Mr Rickaby. William Rickaby. I think he's foreign,' she concluded, slightly perplexed.

Swainson pushed aside Mr Sayed's business and started to rise from the chair. He got half-way out, then froze. He closed his eyes tightly and his arms struggled to support his body. A fast-moving picture unfolded before his eyes. Berlin 1955. A seedy night club. A younger Robert Swainson drunk for the first time in his life. The giddy, pulsating music, the heavy smoke, the damp and slimy walls of the cellar bar. And then staggering out alone, vomiting in the alley way, and then the helpful German, the cramped apartment, his head swirling, more drink, faces going in and out of focus, turning and twisting. Then the younger German. Fifteen? Blond-haired and blue-eyed, clear and bright. The bed, and the blond hair matted against a sweaty brow, the boy smiling, then crying.

And then the morning, his head throbbing, vague memories, snatches from the night before. The hurried dash back to barracks. And then nothing, only guilt which haunted him through the last six months of his stay in Germany. Packing up, excited, back to old Blighty. Thoughts of a career. A letter? No, a photograph. Swainson and the young German. In bed together. Naked. Nothing else. Vomiting again as he had done on that night. Back in England a visit from a stranger. He did not want money. He had money for Swainson. And a suggestion. Become an estate agent.

'Are you alright, dear?' asked Anne.

Swainson made it to his feet. 'Got up a little too quickly. Dizzy,' he said, rubbing his forehead. 'Show him in, would you.' She looked at him, a frown creasing her brow, as if unsure of whether to comply. He smiled at her. 'I'm fine. Ask him to come in.'

He sat down again when she had gone and buried his

face in his hands. 1966. That was the first time he had met Rickaby. September. He had called at the Gloucester Road office. He had wanted Swainson to provide him with three empty houses in three different locations in London. Swainson had done so. Rickaby had said he would only need them for a few days, but he had held onto them until the end of October.

When Swainson had eventually got back the keys, he went round to inspect the houses. Only one of them had been lived in. The headlines in all the newspapers during part of October had been concerned with the escape from Wormwood Scrubs of the Soviet Spy, George Blake. Swainson would have been a fool if he had failed to make the connection.

Rickaby had contacted him on two further occasions, and each time Swainson had provided him with discreet accommodation. The last time had been in the mid-seventies, and since then, not a word. Swainson had forgotten all about Rickaby as he assumed Rickaby had forgotten about him. Until now.

The study door opened. Swainson stood quickly. 'Mr Rickaby for you, Robert,' said his wife.

'Come in, come in,' said Swainson, as he crossed the floor to greet his caller. A knot of fear, of hatred, throbbed away inside. But he showed nothing on the outside except his cool, efficient businessman's face. 'Robert Swainson,' he announced as he shook Rickaby's hand. His wife closed the door on them.

II

'Good?'

'I thought I was supposed to ask that,' said Mercer.

'You are. But you never do,' said Mary, and pinched him just below the ribs.

'Ouch!' said Mercer and moved across to the other side of the bed.

'Come back here.' Mary reached out to him and b[...]
to tug his arm. 'I need a shoulder.' They snuggled up [...]
each other, their bodies, lubricated by the sweat of their
love-making, slipping neatly together in position.
Mercer was drifting off to sleep when the telephone rang.
He gently raised Mary's head from his shoulder and
edged away from her embrace. 'Time you got an ex-
tension,' she murmured.'

Mercer went through into the living-room and picked
up the receiver. It was Todd – angry and drunk – 'You
prick,' he bellowed as soon as soon as he heard Mercer's
voice.

'What's the matter?' asked Mercer.

'Kept me talking and drinking at the party while your
friends went to work. Or was it the other lot? MI5?'

'I don't know what the hell you're talking about,' protested Mercer.

'I bet. My flat was turned over while I was out. The
tapes, all my papers gone. All that hard work . . .'

Mercer interrupted. 'I know nothing about it.'

'Don't give me that, you bastard. If you hadn't have
kept me talking I could have been back home. Probably
caught them at it.'

'Have you considered that if you had caught them at it,
as you say, you'd probably not be in a fit state to call me
now? Or ever, for that matter.' Mercer waited for a reply.
When none came, he continued. 'I had nothing to do
with it, Tom. Honestly. And if you remember rightly, it
was you who were doing all the talking. Not me.'

'They took the lot. Even the rough notes.' Mercer
thought he heard a sob. He was trying to keep calm. He
had only a notion of what was contained in Todd's
papers, and that he had contributed to them. They could
prove highly embarrassing to him in certain hands.

'Anything else taken?' asked Mercer.

'No. They came for the papers and they got them.'

They talked for a while longer, Mercer again
reassuring his friend that he had nothing to do with the

burglary, but refusing to be drawn on the question of who was responsible. The telephone was bugged as far as he was concerned.

He crept silently back to bed, but Mary woke as he got in. 'Who was it?' she asked drowsily.

'Only Tom. Wanted to know whether we got home safely,' he lied.

'Nice of him,' she said and curled up against him. Mercer lay on his back, deep in thought. He had casually mentioned to Mary earlier in the week that he had been invited to a party by an old friend. She insisted that they went. 'You need to get out and about,' she had said. That was true. He had been virtually chained to his desk for weeks, and as the prospect of leaving the Service had faded against the background of the mole hunt, he had become withdrawn and truculent. So they had gone to the party.

He was glad he had. There had been plenty of drink and lots of good food which his waist-band needed. Todd had welcomed them and introduced them around. Many of the other guests were involved in journalism and the theatre, and Mercer had done a lot of enjoyable listening before Todd had collared him and taken him aside.

The pleasure he had felt during the party, the joy in making love to Mary, had evaporated. He was cold and afraid now. Deep inside a fear lurked, one that had haunted him from the day the first network had been captured. The suspicion at Century House that Mercer was the mole was beginning to take root. He was still being followed wherever he went at night. And who had stolen Todd's papers? The papers that Todd had hoped to turn into a book to expose the Peterhouse Mafia. Department F2(R) of MI5 oversaw the activities of British journalists, especially those such as Todd, who had left-wing leanings. MI5 could have been responsible. But somehow Mercer didn't think so.

He sensed that the theft had been directed at him rather than Todd, that the papers were to be used against

130

him. But by whom? Cameron and Fordyce? Why? His thoughts were interrupted by Mary who began to snore gently. He kissed her fondly on the top of the head and stroked her hair. He was lost and confused. One way or the other, it seemed that he was going to be tied to the Service for some time yet.

He thought about going to see the Old Man. To talk about it with him. He hadn't seen him for a few weeks. He'd been too caught up in what was happening around him. But the Old Man was up and about now. Fit and well. Todd had told him at the party that the Old Man was going back to work. Not for the Service, but for Airwork Industries, as a consultant. Mercer had been pleased with the news, but Todd had been very scathing and cynical without explaining why. He would go and see the Old Man as soon as he had the time to spare.

London, England

I

Abdulatif Merza, a junior diplomat at the South Yemeni People's Embassy, drove his Datsun Cherry with CD plates out of Queen's Gate, along Kensington Gore and into Kensington Road. It was ten-fifteen and the traffic was normal for that time of night. He reckoned he would arrive on time, give or take the odd minute or two.

He kept to the inside lane as much as possible and held his speed below forty. Into Knightsbridge, then left at Hyde Park Corner and along Park Lane. Just before he reached the junction with Grosvenor Gate, he swung the car into the entrance to the underground car park

He went down one level, heading in the direction of Speaker's Corner. All of the parking spaces were filled. But just as he seemed to be running out of space, a green Audi vacated its spot in front of him. Abdulatif nipped in smartly. He locked all the doors and the boot and went in search of the exit.

Half an hour later, Todor Zarev ambled along the concrete walkway, car keys in his hand. He stopped next to a Volvo saloon and quickly opened the boot. He took a long look round, and with another key, opened the boot of the Datsun Cherry parked next door. He lifted out two black, leather cases, one after the other. Both were marked with the South Yemen's diplomatic seal. The transfer was completed, he slammed both boots closed, climbed into the Volvo and drove off.

II

'Bastards. Bastards,' cursed Zarev. Before him lay the two diplomatic pouches. He had already checked through the drugs and was satisfied. There was no problem with the three assault guns and their ammunition. But the Berettas. He swore again. His practised eye had spotted the trouble immediately. 'Those fucking idiots at Centre,' he raved. He picked up one of the hand guns. It was what he had ordered: a Beretta Lungo Parabellum, 9mm, with the light alloy body. Fine. But the ammunition? It was .22 calibre. Made for the American market for the Plinker and Minx models. Bastards.

He rubbed the top of his bald pate. Useless. He stacked the unwanted magazines to one side. He could not contact Moscow Centre now. It was too late. He would have to find his own ammunition for the guns.

'Pimlico,' he said out loud. He recalled the address from among the list of fall-backs. He would have to go there first thing in the morning.

Rome, Italy

I

Luca Franchi was having the time of his life. He hadn't been home for two days, and if his money held out, he would stay away for another two. He laughed to himself then drank a toast to his mother-in-law. It was she, after all, he explained to the fat, black-haired whore seated at his table, who was responsible for his good fortune. He did not explain further to the girl how this had occurred. But she was not at all interested in his domestic situation, her main concern being the thick wad of notes in Luca's pocket and how she could relieve him of it without having to go to bed with him again.

She signalled the waiter to bring another jug of wine then turned her attentions to Franchi who was fatter than herself and who stank of old sweat and urine. He was unshaven and the front of his shirt was marked with blotches of food and drink. He was a slob, she thought. But he had money.

Franchi stood and staggered to the urinal. His aim was poor and he collided with the door jamb. He eventually made it to the toilet, but his aim had not improved any, and he pissed all over his dusty shoes. Drops of urine wetted his trousers and some dribbled over his hands. He staggered out and back to the table.

The girl tried to fill his glass but he pushed her away. He screwed up his eyes and tilted his head to one side as if to try and focus better on his companion. His lips curled and he swore at her. 'Fucking whore,' he snarled and pushed himself to his feet. He reeled over to the bar and shouted for attention. 'How much?' he asked of the thin barman as he fumbled his wad onto the bar. The whore sidled up to his shoulders drawn, like iron to a magnet, by the sight of the banknotes.

134

Franchi paid up then shoved his way past the girl – out onto the pavement. The barman shrugged at the girl and went to serve another customer. The girl stood in the middle of the bar room, contemplating her next move. She had spent time with that drunken slob and he owed her for that.

Meanwhile, Franchi was in search of more fun. He passed a few bars, peering in through windows and doors, but they were practically empty. Nothing there for him, so he continued down the street, all the while grinning to himself at his good luck. If his mother-in-law hadn't come to stay, he wouldn't be here now, having such a good time. She had sided with his wife the other morning when he had decided to take the day off work because he felt ill. He had a hangover. He had taken it out on the children, the screaming brats, and the two women had ganged up on him. His mother-in-law had actually punched him in retaliation.

He had left the house for work, still feeling bad, but fuming with anger from his treatment at the hands of the women. And he had carried his temper to his work place, Rome International Airport. He had glared menacingly at the arriving passengers. And because of that, because he was working out his temper on all the passing faces, he saw a face he knew. A face he recognised from the photograph album, a new one that had only recently been inserted. It had taken a few seconds for it to register, but he was sure. He ducked away from the barrier and went over to the cigarette shop near the exit, just as the face calmly took its place in the taxi rank queue. The man behind the counter had listened and noted the face, then Luca had returned to take up his position again.

That afternoon, as the shift was finshing, the man in the cigarette shop had called him over. They were very pleased with Franchi and were giving him a few days off. They also had a bonus for him. The man slipped him an envelope and so had begun Franchi's bout of freedom and fun.

135

The last bar on the block was deserted, too. Franchi stood on the corner wondering which way to go. There were a few more bars straight on, but more likely, his drink-sodden brain told him, they would be as dead as the others. He turned left up the alleyway having decided on the bar in the parallel street where he had first met the girl. There was always something going on there, he chuckled to himself.

The alley was dark but the bright lights of the bar on the next corner showed him the way and he staggered forward. He was almost there, almost within the umbrella of yellow and red light spawned by the hanging signs. He was still grinning to himself. Then the light began to wobble. It turned a deep red, then a shuddering black, as he pitched forward unconscious onto the hard ground. The fat whore dropped the brick with which she had struck Franchi and dived for the pocket that bulged with the money that was now all hers.

II

'Fucking idiots,' said the man and threw Tawfiq's photograph onto the pile in front of him.

'They didn't have a chance. The car came flying out of a side street and rammed them.'

'If I told you once, I told you a dozen times, that guy was to have a code Red surveillance.' He picked up the photograph of Tawfiq again and shook it at his second-in-command. 'And that means two cars at least.'

'But that would've meant taking a team off the PLO goons.'

'We know them. Know all about them.' Again he shook the picture at the man. 'It's this guy we don't know anything about. Except that we had him years ago in Al Farrah. Since then, nothing. Until he turns up in Malta on a Libyan passport.'

'Well, they're all out looking for him now.'

'Too bloody late. He's probably out of the country.' He slammed his fist down onto his desk. 'I go away for a couple of hours. And then this. You know what Tel Aviv are like about new faces. They'll be jumping all over me tomorrow when I report this.'

'We still might pick him up.'

'Yeah. And the PLO might sue for peace.' He shook his head resignedly. 'Tell them to keep looking, anyway. I'll be at home all evening if anything happens. And bloody well keep me informed.'

III

Tawfiq had spotted the tail as soon as the taxi got onto the autostrada to Rome. At first he wasn't sure whether the red Fiat was following him or the black limousine up ahead which had left the airport at the same time as he had. But when the limousine had turned off into the suburbs, the Fiat had stayed with him, never more than two cars behind, and it had accompanied the taxi all the way to Tawfiq's hotel.

He wasn't worried about it. He had expected some sort of surveillance. After all, he was travelling on a Libyan passport, having come directly from the People's Bureau in Sliema. He guessed it was the Israelis, but equally it could be the Italians.

He had been glad to get out of Malta. He thought he had been sent there by Colonel Qada in preparation for some mission but all he had done was routine office work, helping with translations and keeping checks on Libyan exiles in that part of the world. All his training, he felt, had been for nought, and he had been desperate to get away. And now, at last, he was getting what he wanted, a chance to strike back at the Israelis. He knew that this did not necessarily entail killing individual Israelis: Israel and her American supporters were all part of the world-wide conspiracy against the Arab people,

137

and any action, anywhere in the world, that struck at this conspiracy was a worthwhile endeavour.

He had stayed in his hotel for two days, venturing out on the third to do some sight-seeing. He was aware of the surveillance at all times. It made him feel slightly uncomfortable but he stuck to the arranged plan. On the fourth day, a car called for him. It drove him through the centre of the city, using the narrow back streets, only occasionally crossing the main roads. There was only one car following him. Then, as his car drove down a narrow, winding street, another suddenly raced from a side-street and rammed the car that had been following him. His driver then accelerated away, leaving the crash and the surveillance far behind.

At a safe house, he shaved off his straggling beard and trimmed his moustache to a few hairs that sprouted directly below both nostrils. That night he was taken by car to Naples where, after a day's delay, he shipped out as an ordinary seaman aboard a cargo vessel bound for Cyprus.

He left the ship in Cyprus and was taken to Limmasol where he was introduced to his new family, which consisted of a young woman of twenty and a child of nine months who Tawfiq was told to call Mohamed. Tawfiq's passport now said he was Muneer Ali Badawi of Cairo. He had been married for just over two years to his wife, Badr, a native of Alexandria, who was his one and only.

To his suprise, and later delight, he found her a very good wife. She played her role to perfection, performing all the tasks and duties of a wife as prescribed by Arab custom. She was a native of Lebanon but had been under the tutelage of the Syrians since she was ten. She had been passed onto the Libyans some time before and had been used in a similiar capacity on another mission. The child had been the result. The child was a bonus when it came to giving an agent cover, the veneer of familiar respectability, when travelling abroad. She would not take part in Tawfiq's mission, but would merely act as a diversion, together with the child, when crossing international frontiers.

The family travelled to Alexandria by ferry at the end of the week, and the following day, they motored down to Cairo, staying overnight at the Heliopolis Sheraton. In the early hours of the next day, they boarded the British Airways flight to London.

London, England

Except for a brief appearance at the Earls Court flat, he had left Rickaby to deal exclusively with Swainson, and that part of the operation was progressing smoothly. Now he was waiting to hear from Ashcroft. He sat at the table in the dingy living room reading a novel he had found in the bedroom, occasionally grinning to himself at the sexual antics of the hero. He had searched the flat from top to bottom and there was nothing that could possibly connect him with Ashcroft in the place. He had surprised himself in the bathroom as he was replacing the bath panel: he had turned and caught sight of himself in the mirror fixed to the back of the door. His heart had skipped a beat as he stared back at his own bald-headed reflection.

He started to skim quickly through the book, looking for the raunchy passages, in the hope of getting to the end before the man returned. But it was a thick novel which, towards the end, was one continuous sexual fantasy. He had not finished when he heard footsteps on the landing outside.

Ashcroft pushed the door open and started to come in. He still had hold of the key in the lock when he came to a sudden halt at the sight of Todor Zarev sitting there at the table. Zarev put the book to one side and beckoned the man to come in. Slowly and suspiciously, Ashcroft removed the key and let the door swing closed. Zarev smiled up at him.

'How did you get in?' asked Ashcroft.

'Same way as you did,' laughed Zarev, and held out his hand. Ashcroft shook it but kept his distance. Zarev could see the suspicion etched in the young man's features. 'Change of plans,' lied Zarev. Ashcroft cocked his head to one side. 'Nothing important,' continued Zarev. 'But better face to face than on the telephone.'

Ashcroft slipped out of his jacket and went on a tour of his domain.

He returned a few minutes later. 'Brought any money?' he asked, and sat down at the table.

'I'll pay you for what you have done so far and there's another five hundred pounds for the extra work.' Ashcroft liked that, and relaxed a little.

'Good book, eh?' he said, nodding at the table. Zarev agreed. 'Okay, then,' said Ashcroft, after a pause. He dropped a slip of paper in front of Zarev. 'A two-toned green Cortina. Parked in Row D. The car park is straight in front of the terminal and the keys in the magnetic box under the right wing. No problems there.'

'The hotel?'

'The Hilton. Small family room for Mr and Mrs Badawi and child on a two week stay. Okay?'

'Fine.'

'The flat was a bit of a problem. Had to take a six month's lease.' Ashcroft held up his hands to ward off any protests about expenses. 'It was the best I could do without references.' He tossed a set of keys at Zarev. 'Address is there on the key ring, Chilworth Street.'

Zarev toyed with the keys as Ashcroft began to detail expenses.

'I had to use some of my own money,' he said. Zarev nodded. 'You owe me seventy-two pounds. Plus the two thousand you promised.'

'Right,' said Zarev getting to his feet. He pulled out a pile of notes from his inside pocket and put it on the table, just in front of Ashcroft. He could see the man's fingers itching to get at it. 'You've done well. Count out what I owe you in expenses. And take three grand for your time.' Ashcroft looked up at him. 'Bonus,' said Zarev with a smile. He received one back. Ashcroft set to counting. 'Can I get a glass of water?'

'Eighteen, nineteen.' Ashcroft looked up again. 'Sure. Help yourself,' and returned to the count, all caution having evaporated at the sight of the cash.

Zarev went into the kitchen and ran the tap. He returned to the living room a few seconds later. 'About tomorrow.' Ashcroft held up his hand and waved Zarev away. Stupid man, thought Zarev.

He saw Ashcroft stacking the ten pound notes in bundles of twenty. He kept counting. Zarev walked round the room, apparently disinterested, inspecting the shoddy contents. Ashcroft ignored him completely.

Zarev crossed in front of the table, went to the door, turned and ambled up behind Ashcroft. The man grinned up at him. Zarev turned as if to continue his perambulations. Ashcroft ducked his head into the pile of notes once more, the back of his neck, covered with strands of greasy hair, exposed to Zarev.

Zarev shot him once, the bullet entering at the hairline, causing the hair to part and curl. The only sound had been a plop from the Beretta; the only sound now was a low gurgle, as Ashcroft, his head buried in the scattered notes, gave up the ghost.

Zarev let himself out, leaving the money for the police.

JUNE 1985
Newhaven, England

I

Pavel's speech was slurred. He sipped his pastis and laughed with the rest of the group as Pierre made another reference to the large-breasted woman sitting at the bar. Another round of drinks was called for and Jean-Paul grandly paid for them. Pavel lost his new pastis in the stack that had accumulated at their table; he was still on his second one but was giving the impression that he was keeping pace with his new-found friends who had started drinking as soon as the boat had left Dieppe.

He had seen them come aboad, laughing and joking, determined to enjoy the trip across the Channel. It had taken Pavel, with his native-competence French and a passing aquaintance with the 'Thoroughbred' barely five minutes to be welcomed to the company. He recognised them immediately as racing men: each had a set of binoculars whose straps were weighted down with thick stacks of racecourse passes: Longchamps, Epsom, Hialegh, Laurel, Newmarket, The Curragh, and many, many more. Pavel, too carried a set, similarly adorned. They were off to Epsom this time, for the Derby, and had spent half an hour discussing the form and prospects of this year's entry. Then, with drinks flowing thick and fast, their conversation had degenerated into an examination of the female form, in particular Pierre's favourite at the bar, the well-endowed Englishwoman who seemed to be on her own.

Just before the boat docked at Newhaven, Pierre made an approach to his fancy who rebuffed him with a withering look and a comment on his ancestry. His five companions fell about laughing and he returned to their company a hero, explaining with a Gallic shrug that she had passed up the chance of a lifetime. It had been a good start to what promised to be a great day and they prepared to disembark full of their schoolboyish *joie de vivre*, lavatory humour and alcoholic bravado. John-Paul led the way down the gangway. Pavel, in high spirits like the rest, followed.

Newhaven customs were a formality and Pavel enjoyed a sigh of relief as he slipped undetected into England without having to show any documentation. In the crowds that swarmed through the customs hall, it was simple to give Pierre and his cronies the slip. They had arranged for a small coach to take them direct to Epsom. Pavel made for the train which would carry him to Victoria in time for lunch.

His contact in Paris had arranged everything. Having arrived in Paris two days earlier from Prague and had his Czech passport duly stamped, he had registered both at the airport and hotel which he had left almost immediately. From there he had gone to an apartment in the Rue St George where everything had been set out for him: new identity, clothes and instructions for his immediate arrival in England. Meanwhile, back at the hotel, his place had been taken by another who would leave for Prague the following day.

The train left Newhaven on time. The compartment was full but quiet and he pretended to sleep so as to avoid any contact with his fellow-travellers. He did not like Jackson, the American. Zarev and the Palestinian had causes, as he himself had. Jackson however was in it solely for the money. True, his training was the best, Special Forces on two tours in Vietnam. Then on his return to America, a brief spell with the CIA, but later forced out by the post-Watergate scandals in what the American press had euphemistically dubbed the Halloween Massacre.

The next four years he had spent in the oil industry, working for his father's consulting company: offshore

Tunisia, the North Sea and Saudi Arabia. A reunion with a friend from the Vietnam days, Ben Servil, had brought him to Pierre in Marseilles, an international broker for assassinations. The list of contracts attributed to Jackson was short, but they had all been carried out in a highly efficient manner. The KGB had taken note of the man, and for the last two years had kept tracks on him through his girl-friend, Billy.

Pavel could not complain, really. But he only wished there had been something other than money that had led to Jackson's inclusion in the team.

All the way to Victoria, Pavel rehearsed the procedures and paroles, the addresses, utilising the tradecraft he had revised under Guryanov's tutelage.

When the train pulled into Victoria, he allowed himself to be carried along in the stampede to the ticket-barrier. On the other side, he took a taxi to Bayswater, dropping off half way down Westbourne Terrace, then walking the rest of the way to Chilworth Street where he entered a basement flat.

He locked the door behind him and checked all the rooms. The suitcase was in place under the bed and the fridge stocked with food and a bottle of vodka. He poured himself a drink and took it into the bedroom. He stretched out on the bed and fell asleep, the vodka untouched.

II

It was early evening when he awoke. He undressed and showered, then collected the suitcase whose contents he emptied onto the bed. He replaced them with his own clothes, his French passport and the binoculars. Among the jumble on the bed he found his new British passport, driving license and credit cards. He put them aside, together with the bundle of banknotes and loose change. All the clothes were his size: he dressed in jeans, white shirt and woollen sweater. Inside one of the black shoes was a small bunch of keys. He put them in his pocket.

In the kitchen, he made himself a chicken sandwich and washed it down with a cup of tea. Then he sat down in front of the television, but did not switch it on. He read the week's newspapers stacked in a pile at his elbow and later watched the news and saw highlights of the Derby meeting.

At ten-thirty he donned a light-weight jacket and left the flat. He walked aimlessly for some time through the streets before hailing a taxi which took him to Earls Court. He finally walked to the house that was to be the meeting point for the rest of the team.

Aberdeen, Scotland

The *Fokker Friendship* was barely airborne above Sola airport when the stewardess began doling out the breakfast of cold ham and bread. Jackson refused his meal and asked for a coffee. His drawl was pronounced.

He had flown across to Stavanger from Oslo the previous day where he had had a short stay after his flight from Frankfurt. In Oslo, he had picked up his new identity, Rick Crocker of Corpus Christi, Texas, Drilling Consultant, resident in Norway. He had stayed overnight in a house close to Stavanger's airport at Sola and was now on the early morning shuttle to Aberdeen. Quite a few Americans still lived in Norway, using it as their base to commute to the oilfields in the British, Norwegian and Danish sectors of the North Sea. With the frequent rig moves a consultant could find himself one month in the British sector, the next in the Danish section. In the consultancy game, it was essential to have a permanent base for contacts with the oil companies, and the daily flights between Stavanger and Aberdeen were usually packed to capacity with nomadic oilmen of various nationalities.

Jackson had dressed for the part. He wore a faded denim shirt, jeans and cowboy boots, and around his waist was a wide, brown leather belt with an impressed pattern of loops and whorls. The belt fastened with an oval, cast-brass buckle that dug into his stomach and crotch whenever he bent over or sat. Over his shirt he wore a sleeveless body-warmer of leather with suede shoulder patches, and from the top pocket on the left-hand side protruded two gold Cross biro pens. He had placed his Stetson with a white feather on the brim in the luggage rack, along with his aluminium briefcase. Jackson had let his moustache grow and had purposefully not shaved that morning so that he had a rather

147

shaggy appearance about the face, whose features were blurred and indistinct. On the third finger of the right hand he wore a thick band of gold encrusted with tiny specks of diamond, while the same finger on the left was endowed with a gold puzzle ring topped by a small red ruby.

In the heyday of oil exploration off Aberdeen, Americans dressed as Jackson was now, were a common sight, and while their numbers had fallen off over the years, and the cowboy image had been superceded by fast-talking business-suited types, there were still enough old hands operating in the North Sea for Jackson's appearance to go unnoticed and his identity to go unchallenged.

He had no problems at Immigration, his blue passport and eccentric dress receiving a minimum of attention, and nobody gave him a second glance as he strode through the terminal towards the exit. He might have stood out like a sore thumb, yet he was invisible, his clothes a mask of anonymity.

In the car park, he found the green Cortina in Row D: the keys were in a magnetised box under the right wing.

He headed for Dundee, skirting Aberdeen city centre.

In Dundee, he parked the car at the railway station and boarded the Bristol train carrying the suitcase from the boot. At Preston he got off and went straight to the toilet. He threw away his ticket, and changed his boots for a pair of grubby track shoes, and covered his shirt with a heavy blue sweater. He collected his money and passport, then locked up the case. He just had time to eat a sandwich in the buffet before the London train pulled in. He bought a ticket and boarded.

The nearer he got to London, the more excited he got. He could feel it in his stomach. This was the last one, he told himself – the big pay day. When this job was over, he could afford to retire to Holland with Billy. He smiled to himself. She had not been upset this time as he had told her this was the last one. She had believed him and had

148

been overjoyed by the prospect of Holland. There was only one thing that worried him. He was not going it alone on this job. There were three other guys involved. He would have to be careful. Watch himself. Cover his ass. But he had a feeling everything was going to be alright. His real future with Billy was about to begin.

Heathrow, England

I

Wilson's feet were hot and swollen. He knew what they would look like when he took off his shoes that evening. The skin would show the pattern of his knitted woollen socks which would smell of the sweat of a full twenty-four hours. He was desperately tired, having been up all night on the twilight shift, and now, a little before midday, when he should have been at home in bed, he was still working, his relief having failed to show up.

He had called Lacey to report this, but the photographer had been unable to help. All that he could do was to arrange for someone to relieve Wilson that evening. Which was not much good to the sleepy Wilson. The night had been slow and boring as very few flights came his way. Since dawn, the arrivals had increased as the daily traffic climbed to its peak and his eyes were tired and strained; and he longed for the comfort of sleep.

There was a pause in the flow of arriving passengers and Wilson decided to risk a visit to the bathroom. He propped his board against the barrier and took off. He washed his hands and face, and, with his ablutions over, he strolled across to the coffee machine. He stood there drinking the coffee, and it was a few minutes before he saw that there were passengers coming through the gate. He dropped the polystyrene cup in the bin and strode back to take up his position, glancing over at those travellers who had come past his vantage point while he had been drinking coffee. There were no faces there he recognised, and so he turned his attention to those who were now emerging.

After a while, his eyes began to get tired again. He rubbed them and saw multi-coloured patterns before them, and he had to blink several more times to get his vision under control. Then he nearly missed him. It was the child, bleating, and twisting in its mother's arms that drew his attention to the small group. The mother wore a pink flowered dress that reached down to her ankles and Wilson had put her down as an Arab right away. The baby twisted its little body and screamed. But the husband, the child's father, what was it about him? He wore slacks and a sweater and he was pushing the trolley containing their luggage. The baby was nearing hysteria. The mother tried to comfort him, but the child was beyond simple words of endearment. And the father? Embarrassed? Yes, thought Wilson. Embarrassed. He had seen children react like this before after a long plane journey, and he knew Arab men and women to be most solicitous towards children, even towards those of complete strangers, particularly when the child was upset.

But this man didn't seem to care. Hadn't even tried to help his wife who was now struggling with the infant. The man seemed as if he wanted to get away from it all, to escape. People were now staring at the couple and the baby. The mother decided to ignore the crying child and took up the faster pace being set by her spouse. Strange, thought Wilson. He sidled along the barrier to keep the couple in view, something egging him on. The man's face. Angry and sheepish at the same time, his body straight and rigid. The face . . . Yes, the face.

The skimpy moustache. Yes, that was it. But there was no mistaking the face. It was one of the new ones. He had seen the face when it was younger without the moustache. The photographs were black and white – from police files – he had guessed.

Wilson reached down into his right-hand pocket and pushed the on button of his transmitter. He saw the man sitting on a bench, reading a newspaper, a suitcase at his feet. The man slowly raised his eyes above the top of the paper and began to scan the milling crowd, like a dog suddenly aware of a new scent on the air. Wilson spoke into the badge pinned to his lapel and watched as the man fingered his hearing-aid. Then the man got to his feet and picked up his case, leaving the newspaper on the bench. Wilson made for the exit, weaving his way through the crowd, keeping about ten yards between himself and the Arab family with the wailing infant.

II

On the way into London, Badr avoided his eyes. She sat in one corner of the taxi, her arms wrapped around her son, who sobbed quietly to himself. Tawfiq was white with fury. His fists were clenched tightly and his mouth was set firm, while his eyes blazed into the back of the driver's head.

She had told him on the plane that the child was not well, that this journey was too soon after the ferry ride to Alexandria. But he had ignored her, thinking she was just being too much of a mother. But as they had disembarked from the plane, the child had started its bleating. Tawfiq had been unsure of what to do. He simply let her get on with it. As they came through customs, he had got angrier as the crying continued. He tried to comfort the baby, but his face must have given him away as Badr would not let him near her son. Stupid bitch.

She had probably given the game away there and then. When they came out into the arrivals hall, the child was almost hysterical; he couldn't help, and even Badr was getting a little worried, particularly when everyone began staring at them. He had tried to brazen it out, but he knew there was the distinct possibility they had picked up a tail. Too many people had had too much time to look him over as he had pushed their luggage trolley to the taxi rank.

He resisted the temptation to look back out of the window to see if there was anybody following. If there was anybody behind, they would be alerted by Tawfiq's movement and he didn't want to do that. If he had a tail he didn't want them to know that he knew. Then they might get a little complacent and careless, and be unprepared for the moment when he would make his move. And that, he decided, would be as soon as possible.

London, England

I

Stern went into the lobby of the Hilton and casually made his way towards the bank of lifts. He passed within a few feet of Tawfiq at the registration desk where he was filling in forms. The girl stood to one side holding the baby who was now asleep. He watched as Tawfiq's luggage was collected by the bell-boy – and moved directly in front of the lift doors along with two or three other guests, as Tawfiq and the girl arrived.

He was the first into the lift and he stood in a corner at the back as it filled up. He saw the bell-boy press several buttons on request and he stayed in the car until the seventh floor; Tawfiq got off at the sixth. Stern saw the key in the bell-boy's hand. They were staying in Room 619.

He returned to the reception and met up with Robson. 'Muneer Ali Badawi and wife,' said Robson. 'Got it from the passenger list.'

'Okay. They're in Room 619. Let's see if we can get one nearby.'

II

Badr tucked the baby into the cot. Tawfiq sat on the bed and picked up the telephone and dialled the number. He spoke rapidly in Arabic for several seconds, paused while he listened, then spoke again before hanging up. He went over to the luggage rack and pulled out his suitcase which he took into the bathroom. He stripped off, showered, then dressed again in fresh clothes from the suitcase. He smoothed out the creases as best he could then went back into the room. Badr was stretched out on the bed, her eyes closed. He opened the door and saw the corridor was empty.

Using the fire stairs he went down to the fourth floor, and was admitted after one knock to Room 409. Nobody saw him enter.

III

Stern was getting worried. The occupants of Room 619 had not been out since their arrival, thirty-six hours beforehand. He had been lucky to get Room 617 and Robson and Sophie had set up shop there. The wall mikes said the man and woman with the child were still inside, and he learnt from one of the cleaners that the baby was ill and that the parents were scared to go out with it in case it got worse.

Could be, reasoned Stern, but he was nevertheless worried. This guy had proved a slippery customer back in Rome, and Stern was determined that he would not give him the slip. But short of bursting in on them, there was little to do but wait for them to come out.

And come out they did on the third day. Stern saw them emerge from the lift from his vantage point in the mezzanine lounge, and his heart skipped a beat. He screwed up his eyes and studied the face of the man. He was not sure. The girl was okay. But the man? He watched them approach the reception desk. The man was talking to the clerk. The clerk handed over a folder which the man opened. Stern wondered if they were checking out, though they had registered for a two week stay. Robson joined him.

The man took out a pen and began to write. Stern's heart sank. 'The bastard's done it again,' he whispered to Robson.

'What d'you mean?'

'He's gone. That's not him.'

Robson leant forward for a better look. 'Are you sure?'

'Course I'm sure. Fuck me. Let's go.' He pulled Robson by the arm. 'Come on. That guy's writing left-handed. Our man signed in with his right.'

IV

Superintendent Walsh's view from the seventeenth floor of the New Scotland Yard building was decidedly ugly, and he never tired of telling his Sergeant that his only interest in promotion was to gain an office further along the corridor and round the corner where the outlook from the hatch, that was laughingly called a window, was a slight improvement. He stared down at the roof of Victoria Station, coated with the grime of decades and wrinkled his nose. 'Dirty place,' he said out loud just as a tap sounded on his door. 'Come,' he said over his shoulder and continued gazing.

'Morning, sir,' said Pigott.

'I suppose we're lucky, really,' said Walsh with a sigh.

'Sir?'

'No smog,' said Walsh turning around and seating himself at his desk. Pigott looked bemused. 'If we were in Los Angeles,' continued Walsh, 'we'd be lucky if we could see ten yards what with all the smog that makes it the coughing capital of the world.'

'That's where the Olympics were held.' Pigott began running on the spot.

'I get the picture, Tom.' He sat back in his seat and looked at his Sergeant. Both men fell silent and a minute passed before Walsh spoke again. 'Well?'

Pigott shook his head. 'Well what, sir?' He tried a smile but it was met by an impatient snarl.

'I take it you didn't come in here to tell me about the Olympics, eh?'

'Oh no,' said Pigott, trying the smile again. Walsh looked to the ceiling in exasperation. Pigott had only been with him for six months and so far had shown little skill in detecting the quirky moods that periodically overcame his superior. Walsh prayed that he showed more aptitude for the work he was paid to do.

'Well then,' said Walsh waving a hand at Pigott, giving the man the signal to begin, much in the same way a starter commenced a race with a flag.

'Right. Er. I was talking to Sergeant Hutchinson this morning, and . . .'

'Was he the individual I saw you with at the lifts when I came in?'

'Yes, sir.'

'He's not with Special Branch, is he?'

'No sir. CII. Surveillance.'

'Criminal Intelligence,' said Walsh, his eyes narrowing. 'We don't have anything to do with that lot, Sergeant. Too much of the former, not enough of the latter.'

'I've heard that one before,' said Pigott with a grin.

'It's not meant to be funny at all Sergeant. I don't like my men even passing the time of day with any of that gang.'

'Sergeant Hutchinson's okay, sir. Decent bloke, actually. His father . . .'

'Spare me the details. Keep away from them. Hutchinson included.'

'Yes sir,' said Pigott. He began to shuffle his feet and look around the room.

'Go on then,' prompted Walsh.

'Sir?'

'Come off it, Tom. What do you want to tell me?' He fixed his Sergeant with a beady stare.

'Oh, he thought he might have something for us.'

'Really.'

'A man named Tomlinson. Into everything. They give him the once over now and again.'

'Especially when it's getting near the summer holidays, eh?'

'If you say so, sir. Anyway, they had been giving him a

157

look over: they thought he was acting a little suspiciously. Then two nights ago, he winds up dead in Hackney. Shot in the back of the neck.'

Walsh frowned and rubbed his chin. 'The back of the neck, you say.' Walsh got to his feet and returned to the window. 'And why did Hutchinson think this man's death should interest us?'

'He said it looked like a Russian execution.'

Walsh spun round on his heels, a huge smile on his face. 'A Russian one? And what distinguishes a Russian murder from a British or an American one? Or even one from Outer Mongolia?'

'The single shot in the back of the neck. Hutchinson says the Russians are noted for it.'

'Is that it, then? A Russian murder.'

'Well, yes. Except that I ran through our files. We've got Tomlinson in a red file.' Walsh frowned. 'An alias of course. We've got him down as William John Rickaby. He . . .'

'He's got known connections with the Russians. I know.'

'Didn't we have him in here a few weeks ago, after that tip-off from CI3?'

'Our Mr Rickaby has been in here quite a few times over the years. Especially in his role as legman for some of the Soviet Embassy hoods.' Walsh cracked his knuckles, his features deep in concentration. 'Okay, Sergeant. Get back to your friend Hutchinson. Find out all about the man's death. Particularly the calibre of the bullet and the make, if possible!'

'Right away, sir,' said Pigott, making for the door.

'And Sergeant. Make it some time today.' Pigott left the room. Walsh collected his briefcase from the floor and lifted it up on to his desk. He took out the notes he had made at the Interpol conference earlier that year, together with the case histories of suspected assassins which Interpol had put together for the visiting Police Officers. He also removed two reports he had picked up ealier that morning from the Pathology Department. Perhaps his labours of the last few days had not been in vain.

He spent half an hour checking details. There was the murder of a man named Ashcroft in Camden last week, which had followed the death of a suspected arms-trafficker in Pimlico. Both men had died with a single shot to the back of the neck. The weapon in both cases had been a 9mm calibre Beretta. Rickaby's death could make it three.

The Interpol case histories threw up one man. Fat and balding according to the grainy photograph. Name: Todor Zarev. Occupation: KGB hit-man. An expert in wet affairs. He picked up his phone. Lewis at MI5? He thought for a minute. His policeman's instinct told him no. He dialled Mercer's number at Century House.

Chiddingfold, England

I

'First made in 1951 for special detachments of the Italian Airforce. Ergal body, magazine holds ten rounds.' Zarev held up one of the Berettas, and pulled back the slide on top of the barrel. He pointed the gun and fired at the wall opposite. The plop of the discharge was almost swallowed by the sound of the bullet hitting the wooden panel. Pavel sniffed at the harsh smell of cordite. 'The charge in each cartridge has been reduced to cut down the noise. Don't worry about range or stopping power. Use the Beretta for close work only.'

Pavel was watching Jackson and Tawfiq. The American appeared at ease, but the Palestinian was all eyes, darting here and there, reluctant to rest, insisting on keeping everybody in sight. 'Heckler and Koch. MP5K,' continued Zarev, as he turned his attention to the machine pistols. Tawfiq was staring at Pavel. Zarev stopped his narrative as he stripped down the weapon. Pavel gave Tawfiq a friendly smile. Tawfiq glared back.

II

Jackson tried to keep his mind on what Zarev was doing, but he was too aware of the agitated Palestinian at his side. The man was as taut and finely tuned as a concert harp – bristling and burning with energy. Jackson didn't like that at all. He had seen that kind of tension, of battle-readiness, in men during his time in Vietnam. Men ready to explode into action. They usually ended up tripping over their own feet, or shooting one of their own comrades in their eagerness to get on with it, before getting shot themselves. A good dose of fear, thought

Jackson, was all that was needed before a fight. He would ensure that the Palestinian was in front of him when the fun began.

III

Tawfiq didn't trust any of them. The American in particular. He was too relaxed. Or seemed to be. He never looked at anyone's face. He kept his eyes at chest level, and was always wary of where the others were. He stood with his back to the wall whenever possible. No. The American didn't trust anybody either. But he hid it well.

Tawfiq stared at the Russian who looked away to watch Zarev stripping down the machine pistol. The Russian seemed to be okay. But Zarev? He had death written all over him.

IV

Zarev noticed the exchange between Pavel and Tawfiq. The Palestinian would have to go first. He was more likely to cause problems. He would use the American to kill him. Then he and Pavel could eliminate the American when it suited them. 'Right,' concluded Zarev. 'Tawfiq. Jackson. Come up here. Pick out your weapons.' The two men came forward to the table. 'Doctor. Next door with me. I want you to check over your medicines.' He smiled. He also wanted to tell Pavel how they were going to get rid of Jackson and Tawfiq when Golden Fleece was successfully completed.

London, England

I

Swainson was ill again. He went through into his private toilet and bent over the sink. His stomach heaved but it was empty. It could not repeat the emission of the watery goo and gunk that had erupted into the sink an hour earlier. Swainson could still taste it in his mouth, and he retched again. A trickle of bile ran from his lips and dripped onto the porcelain, burning the back of his mouth as it passed through. He lowered himself onto the toilet seat and turned on the tap in the sink. He allowed the water to run over his fingers for a few seconds before dabbing some of it on his flushed face. He felt a little better.

He stood and drank some of the water before turning off the tap. He carefully avoided his reflection in the mirror, afraid to see the face of a dead man. He staggered back into his office and sagged into the nearest chair. He was a dead man, he told himself. There was no mistake. The folded newspaper on his desk said it all. The one he had picked up at lunchtime on his way back to the office. On the front page was a picture of Rickaby. Only the newspaper called him Tomlinson. No matter. It was definitely Rickaby. And he was dead. Yesterday morning they had found him, shot in the back of the neck. Swainson shuddered at the thought.

He could guess who was responsible for Rickaby's murder. The fat, bald man whom Rickaby had brought along last week when Swainson had met him to show him round the flat in Earls Court. An evil-looking man, Swainson had thought on first sight. And how true that impression had turned out to be. For the same fat, bald man was outside Swainson's office right now. Across the road, sitting in his car. Waiting for him. Waiting to kill him.

162

Swainson had sensed there was something different about this latest contact with Rickaby. The man had been tense throughout, very particular about the accommodation Swainson had offered, even to the extent of allowing another person, the fat, bald man the final say in the selection. Rickaby had not done that before. And then there were the plans of the house down in Godalming. Something which Swainson had never been asked to supply before. And the trouble Swainson had had in getting them. No. There was something definitely wrong.

Rickaby's death proved that. Someone was making sure there weren't any witnesses to his and Rickaby's dealings. The fat man outside. Swainson had spotted him when he stopped to buy his newspaper. Just a glimpse, but he recognised him. He had seen him get into the car from his office window. He had checked again, an hour later, and he was still there.

Swainson felt drowsy and so allowed himself the luxury of a short catnap. His secretary woke him up. She was going home. It was close to five-thirty. He couldn't hide in his office forever, but if he didn't leave shortly, he was sure the fat man would come in looking for him. He had to think. He couldn't just sit there like a caged animal waiting for the death blow. He had to get away. He suddenly remembered a way out.

He went to the wall safe and opened it. He took out all the papers and documents and then removed the back panel. A second, smaller safe was revealed. From it he took a bundle of five pound notes, and the false passport that Rickaby had supplied him with years ago. The photograph showed a much younger Swainson. The passport still had three years of life. He put it in his briefcase along with the money. Another idea came to him.

He went down to the ground floor, to the caretaker's booth, and spoke to Woods about some extra cleaning he wanted doing around the office that evening. The caretaker said he would oblige. Swainson turned to go and then stopped as if struck by a thought. 'I didn't call my wife, did I?' He smiled at the caretaker 'Mind if I use your phone, Mr Woods?'

'Not at all, sir.'

Swainson called Anne at home. He explained that he had a late appointment and that he wouldn't be back home until eleven that night. He hung up and thanked Woods. 'Right. I'll see you in the morning. Is the side door open?'

'Yes, sir. I leave it open for the chars.'

'Good. I'll go out that way. More chance of getting a cab if I cut through onto Cromwell Road.' He said goodnight to Woods and made his way out via the side exit. He just hoped and prayed that the fat man was working alone and that he only had the front entrance covered. Otherwise he was a dead man.

II

The sign in the window of the bookshop said closed. Commander Walsh rang the bell. A thin wedge of light appeared at the back of the shop followed by the outline of a man who shuffled between the rows of books up to the door. He peered through the glass, eyeing Walsh suspiciously. Walsh rang the bell again. 'Alright. Alright. I'm coming already.'

'Stop pissing about Anver. Open the bloody door,' said Walsh. The door swung inwards as the last bolt was withdrawn.

'It's you,' said the Jew.

'Who were you expecting? Yassar Arafat?' Walsh pushed his way inside.

'Funny,' said Anver. He smiled and held out his hand. 'You know the way.' Walsh headed for the light coming from the office. Anver relocked the door before following him. The office walls were lined with books. Walsh was scanning the shelves as Anver entered. 'For you, Commander, a special price. Two for the price of one.'

Walsh turned his attention to Anver. He saw he was dressed in a pair of baggy corduroys, and a grey shirt over which hung a hand-knitted cardigan that had seen too many washes and whose leather elbow patches were cracked and faded. On his feet he wore a pair of ragged carpet slippers that matched the colour of his trousers: greasy brown. Walsh had never seen him dressed any other way in the three years that Anver had been Mossad's chief in London. He was of average height, medium build, and when he wore his horn-rimmed spectacles and left a couple of days growth on his chin, he looked weak and vulnerable, as if he couldn't hurt a fly. Walsh knew him for what he was: a highly trained intelligence agent who had killed on more than one occasion for his country, and would do so again should it be asked of him. 'Why the act? The alright, already bit?'

'I didn't have my glasses on. Besides, I'm feeling particularly Jewish these days.' Walsh plucked a book from the shelf. 'Not for you, my boy,' he added, as he saw Walsh's eyebrows arch. 'Victorian erotica.'

Walsh replaced the volume and continued browsing. 'Going home, are we?'

'Very good, Commander. Next week, in fact. My youngest son. It's his barmitzvah. Hence the retreat into my natural Jewish personality.'

'What are you up to, Anver?' Walsh went across to the window. He could not see out. At first he thought it was dirt, then realised that the glass had been painted over with black paint.

'I'm up to something? A bookseller minding my own business?'

Walsh turned back to face the Israeli. 'Cut it out. I haven't got the time. Milt Tern and Jacob have been tear-arsing around London for the past couple of days. Lose something did they?'

165

Anver straightened himself up and pursed his lips.
'Why?'

'Why what?'

'Why do you want to know?'

Walsh paused for a moment before replying. 'It's my job to know. It's my job to keep track of all hoods and goons operating in our fair land.' Walsh realised he'd made a mistake.

'Hoods. Goons. My people aren't hoods. Goons either,' shouted Anver angrily. 'If it wasn't for my people keeping tabs on all that Arab muck, London would be a bloody shooting gallery.'

'Hold on, Anver. I wasn't referring to your men as goons. But you're certainly after somebody. Why all this activity? I want to know who you are chasing.' Walsh kept his voice even.

'Why?'

'God dammit,' swore Walsh. He knew he had reached an impasse with the Israeli. He wouldn't get any more out of him until he gave a little first. 'Just tell me if he's Russian or not. And don't say who.'

Anver took a seat and invited Walsh to do likewise. 'He's not Russian. Palestinian.' He leant across Walsh and opened a drawer in the table that served as a desk. 'Came into Heathrow three days ago. He got away from us in Rome after we had spotted him coming in from Malta.' He handed a photograph to Walsh. 'Got away from us again at the Hilton.'

'What've you got on him?'

'Not much at all. It's all on the back of the photograph.'

'So why all the interest?' he asked and handed back the snapshot.

'There's something going down. We know next to nothing about him. He hasn't figured in anything at all. Except for that brief period of detention. It's just the way it was all set up.'

'How do you mean?'

166

'The way he broke our surveillance in Rome was timed right down to the last second. And the set-up when he got to London. It's all been too carefully planned. There has to be a reason.'

'Going after your Ambassador again?' suggested Walsh.

Anver shook his head. 'No. It doesn't feel like a Palestinian job at all. It's not their style. Too professional for them.' He rubbed his chin with both hands and closed his eyes. 'Tell me. Why did you think we were after a Russian?'

'I didn't really. But there's one on the loose right now. I thought that perhaps you might have been . . . A long shot.'

'Hmm. When I was in the States the FBI picked up a young Palestinian acting on information I supplied. Let's see. '76. Maybe '77. But he was just like that one in the photograph. We had nothing on him. Never ever involved in the terrorist movement. But suddenly appearing out of the blue. Again in Rome. Ended up in Washington. The FBI reckoned he was working for the Russians. KGB.'

'I see,' said Walsh slowly.

'Could be coincidence,' said Anver, turning both hands palm upwards.

'Could be,' agreed Walsh.'

III

On the wall beside the grey filing cabinet hung a black and white photograph of a group of smiling soldiers. Some were standing, some were sitting cross-legged on the ground, the remainder were stooped on their haunches. They looked young and fresh with their big toothy smiles, close-cropped hair, and loose-fitting battle tunics that had been made for men. But these were boys, still in their teens, eager for life. Commander Walsh was the third face from the left on the back row. He, like the others in the picture, was a National Service soldier. But unlike the others, he survived the UN retreat from the North Korean capital, Pyongyang, when the Chinese overran that city. He had seen most of his mates die on the icy plain; they would never be any older than they were in that photograph. Frozen bodies, frozen time.

Sergeant Pigott was fascinated by the framed picture. He was staring at it for the umpteenth time that day when Commander Walsh breezed into the room. 'Anything?' he asked, as he strode to this desk.

'Nothing on Zarev at all. There's a ballistics report on the desk. He used three different guns for the three killings. Three different Berettas, that is.'

'Sound reasonable,' replied Walsh, picking up the report. 'You buy the guns from Clark in Pimlico, test one on him, a second on Ashcroft and a third on Rickaby. He now knows he has three guns that work without problems.'

'But why would Zarev need three guns?'

'Maybe he has some friends.' Walsh read for a moment. 'Have we got everywhere covered?'

'Yes, sir.'

Walsh suddenly got to his feet. 'Right. I'm off. I'll be at home if anything crops up.' He got halfway to the door when the telephone rang. 'Answer it, Tom.'

'Sergeant Pigott speaking.' He listened for a moment before holding out the receiver to Walsh. 'Sergeant Hern at Heathrow.'

'Yes, Sergeant. What is it?' said Walsh, taking the 'phone.

'We picked up a man at Terminal 3 trying to board a flight using a false passport,' said Hern. 'Man by the name of Robert Swainson.'

Walsh frowned. He put his hand over the mouthpiece and turned to Pigott. 'Swainson?' Pigott shook his head. Walsh put the instrument to his mouth again. 'Okay,

Sergeant. I'll put you through to the Duty Officer. He can deal with it.'

'Excuse me, sir. But this Swainson chap was in a bit of a state. Panic-stricken in fact. Said he was being chased by a Russian spy who was trying to kill him.'

Walsh was just about to say something flippant when a warning bell sounded in his brain. 'Give me all the details, sergeant,' he said sharply.

'Right. We managed to get a description of the guy, the so-called Russian. Fat, bald, below average height.'

'And you showed him Zarev's picture?'

'Yes, sir. No doubt about it.'

'Did he say anything about where Zarev could be located? Or what he's up to over here?'

'We can't shut the guy up. Hasn't stopped talking since we picked him up.'

'The details, sergeant,' said Walsh. Pigott appeared at his side with a pad and pencil. Walsh winked at him.

'I've got three possible places, Sir. Swainson's an estate agent. Zarev's got the keys to two of the places: a flat in Earls Court, and a cottage down near Chiddingfold.' He gave the first two addresses to Walsh who scribbled them down.

'What about the third place?' asked Walsh.

'That could be a blind, sir. Swainson only supplied the plans for that one. No keys.'

'Give it to me anyway,' said Walsh.

'Er. It's a house in Godalming. Shanroe. Just on the outskirts. Yew Tree Lane.'

'Are you sure?' said Walsh. He gripped the receiver tightly and visibly paled.

'Of course . . .'

'Never mind, sergeant. Get Swainson over here pronto. Okay?'

'Right away, sir.'

'And Sergeant. Send two men over to Lacy's. You know the photographic shop in Uxbridge High Street?'

'The Israeli portrait gallery?'

169

'Yes. Bring in all the albums. They're in a cupboard behind a panel under the stairs.'

'What about entry?'

'Use your loaf, man. This is an emergency. Just get the albums. We'll deal with Lacy when the time comes.' He slammed down the 'phone and it rattled in its cradle.

'The Israelis have a better collection of faces than we have,' said Walsh, by way of explanation to Pigott. 'Zarev's not working alone on this. Swainson might be able to pick out someone.'

Walsh sat down and thought for a minute. He produced a small bunch of keys from his trouser pocket and unlocked a drawer in his desk. 'Get hold of the Duty Officer. I want two teams armed and ready to go in five minutes.' He took out a red address book. 'One for the Earls Court address, the other for . . .' He reached for the pad. 'Chiddingfold. Where the hell is that? Chiddingfold?'

'South of Godalming,' said Pigott, walking over to, and pointing at, the wall map.

'Okay,' said Walsh. He opened the book under the letter P. 'A walk-by squad for Swainson's house also. Armed. Move it.' Pigott made a swift exit.

Walsh found the name Plum. There was a telephone number. He dialled it and waited for the connection. All he heard was his own breathing. So he dialled again. The line was dead. He got onto the switchboard. 'Get me the local nick at Godalming. I'll hold.' His fingers drummed out a rhythm on the blotter. 'Hello. Can I have the Station Commander. It's Commander Walsh. Special Branch.' Another pause.

'Inspector Raison speaking. Good evening Commander.'

'You have a Security Blue resident in Yew Tree Lane. His 'phone's dead. This is an Alpha Red Alert. Get your men into that house. I'm sending additional strength . . .'

'Whoa, Commander. Hold on now,' said Inspector Raison. 'Alpha Red Alerts. No, no. Just because his phone is dead? There could be any number of reasons for that. I'll call the house. You've probably had a crossed line. Can't have the balloon go up everytime a line goes down, eh?' He started to laugh.

'Listen, you fucking wind bag. Get your men in there. That's a direct order. The man's life is in danger. D'you think we're idiots or something up in London? Now get off your fat arse and get your men mobile. Armed. Got it?' He threw the 'phone down without waiting for a reply.

'All set,' said Pigott, as he re-entered, his face flushed, and a little out of breath. 'I took the liberty of ordering a team for the Godalming address. Just in case.

'Very good, Tom. I want you to stay here with me. Send them on their way.'

'Right sir. Oh, I've had communications put everything through to you here.'

'Thanks,' said Walsh. He winked at his Sergeant as he left the room. Walsh got to his feet. 'What next?' he asked himself 'The Home Office? Yes.' He started to dial then stopped midway. He called Mercer instead and told him that there was a car on its way to collect him. Then he rang the Home Office.

IV

The telephone rang at the same time as the doorbell chimed. Mercer, coming out of the bedroom after having changed his shirt, was caught in a moment of indecision between the two summonses. He went to the front door as it was nearer. 'Just hang on a minute,' he said to the uniformed policeman. He trotted through into the living room and answered the 'phone.

'What's going on?' snapped Fordyce into Mercer's ear.

'This isn't a secure line,' said Mercer.

'What's happening down at Alex Cameron's place?' The voice was edged with panic.

'We are not secure. Do you understand?'

'The Home Office have just . . .' Mercer put down the 'phone. He collected his jacket from the back of a chair and put it on. He left all the lights on and went out with the police officer.

Mercer sat in the back of the car. Fordyce had wanted to know what was happening. Mercer would have liked to know also. Walsh had called round to see him at Century House late in the afternoon to tell him about Zarev and Mossad's missing Palestinian. Mercer had been unable to see any connection between the two wanted men, but his interest had been aroused by Zarev's presence in Britain. He had wondered if MI5 or the Service had any eastern bloc defectors tucked away somewhere who would be a likely target for Zarev. That seemed to fit. The mole in the Service could have fingered the defector for the KGB and Zarev could have been sent over to teminate the unfortunate person. Could be. But . . .

Walsh had said nothing over the 'phone except to say there was a car on the way. Fordyce, in his hysterical call, seemed to think there was something wrong with Alex Cameron. Mercer closed his eyes and relaxed. A germ of an idea took root. He let it grow and spread. It made him open his eyes quickly. He told the police driver to put his foot down. Mercer was worried. He began to rock back and forth in his seat.

Purley, England

I

The caretaker had overheard Swainson talking to his wife, telling her that he would not be home until eleven o'clock. Zarev had paid the man ten pounds for the information. It was an inconvenience for Zarev. It meant him waiting there, outside the house, for Swainson's return. What was more, he would be late in arriving at the cottage. Pavel and the others would be there by the time he motored down to Worplesdon. But, it couldn't be helped. Swainson was the last of the loose-ends that had to be tidied up for the sake of the operation.

He checked the rear-view mirror. The pavement behind was dark and deserted. Ahead, through the windscreen, he could see the glow of the porch-light of the Swainson home and the rear of the family car protruding from the driveway. Half an hour to go. Swainson would either take a taxi from the station, or call his wife to come and collect him by car. Either way, Zarev would be ready. He very much doubted if Swainson or his wife would survive the night.

A dog barked. Close by. Out of the night came a young couple arm in arm, pulled along by an excited dog that strained at its leash as it sniffed and snorted at gate-post and street light alike. The trio passed by the Swainsons', then Zarev's car, and were swallowed up by the night. Zarev watched them in the mirror until they had gone from view, the occasional bark, distant and muted, marking their position along the street. He relaxed.

II

'Okay,' said Commander Walsh into the telephone. 'Take him. Alive if possible. But don't take any unnecessary risks. He's highly dangerous.' He put down the receiver and gave the thumbs-up sign to Mercer who had just come into his office.

III

Quarter of an hour to go. Zarev decided on one last cigarette. He rolled down his window and lit up. He patted his coat pocket from habit and felt the solid lump of his Beretta. He took a deep drag on his cigarette and the heavy smoke caught the back of his throat causing him to cough. He spluttered and choked for a few seconds before gaining control and another deep drag quelled his protesting lungs. He watched the smoke curl and twist through the open window and he could feel a tiny knot of tension in his gut as the time grew closer.

A dog barked again. The same one as before. He was sure of it. He tossed away his cigarette and sat up straight. Yes. The same trio. He could see them in the rear-view mirror. The dog was a Dalmatian, not fully grown, and frisky and alert as only a young dog in the summer can be. It really had a hold of the leash now and was pulling its master all over the pavement. The woman was having problems hanging on to the man.

The yapping and barking was much louder than before and Zarev was starting to become uneasy. The noise might attract the neighbours; it could alert Swainson if he were to put in an appearance now and prevent Zarev from getting in close enough to deliver the death blows. Zarev kept his eye on the dog. He could hear the man's voice chiding the dog and he mentally urged him to be a lot firmer with his pet. The dog reached the boot of the car and kept on coming. Zarev saw the man's arm and part of his body as he passed the car. The woman followed a few steps behind.

Suddenly, the man shouted. 'Hey.' Zarev saw the dog dash across the front of the car and run over to the other side of the street, the leash trailing on the ground. In that instant Zarev knew he was taken. The man chased the dog across the front of the car. Zarev's right hand dropped to his coat pocket which was hard up against the door. As he twisted his body to get at the Beretta, the man turned sharply and dived for the open window. At the same time there was a tap of metal on glass.

Zarev saw the woman on the passenger side staring deadpan at him, the .38 Smith and Wesson held firmly in both hands, pointing at his head. A second Smith and Wesson entered his vision as the man pushed his weapon through the open window. It came to rest two inches from his temple. 'Police,' shouted the man. 'Get your fucking hands on the wheel.'

Godalming, England

I

Twilight. Shades of grey and blue. The country road looked darker than the surrounding countryside. The green transit van was parked on the bend. From the driver's seat Jackson could just see the gable-end of the house in Yew Tree Lane. There was a light coming from the windows. He leant forward and peered upwards through the windscreen at the telephone pole. He could not see Tawfiq. Then he saw his feet, which almost immediately disappeared from view. He heard them a second later as they landed on the roof of the van. This was followed by a rustling sound in the hedgerow, then Tawfiq's face appeared on the passenger side. He opened the door and climbed in.

'Okay,' said Tawfiq. 'Let's go.' Pavel's hand came from the darkened interior and patted him on the shoulder. Jackson put the van in gear and drove round the curve and up to the front gates of Shanroe. He parked the van so that it blocked the entrance, switched off the engine and pocketed the ignition keys.

'All set?' asked Pavel. Tawfiq and Jackson nodded. They climbed out and silently closed the doors. All three wore jeans and thin, black roll-neck sweaters made of cotton. On their feet they had black running shoes. 'Weapons?' said Pavel. Each man had a shoulder holster which held a Beretta, and they each carried an MP5K with extra magazines tucked into their belts.

They checked their weapons and their ammunition. Pavel passed Jackson a round suction cup like those found in kitchens which are prone to blocked drains. Tied to the wooden handle was a heavy glass cutter. Jackson tucked it under his arm: Pavel did the same with his.

The house was hidden from them behind the tree-lined, curving drive. Stooping low, the three men set off at a trot up the drive on Pavel's order. Jackson broke away from the others first and made for the tennis court. Tawfiq and Pavel continued together until they reached the paved patio at the side of the house. Tawfiq kept on going while Pavel dashed across the flagstones and threw himself flat against the wall. He was less that a foot away from the french windows which were closed and curtained.

Pavel started a mental count. From inside the house he heard the distant chime of a bell which signalled that Tawfiq was at the front door. He crept up to the window and pressed the suction cup hard against the glass. He dug in the glass cutter and cut a circle as he held onto the wooden handle. He thought he heard the sound of footsteps above the noise of the breaking glass.

II

Cameron put down his brandy glass and frowned. He cocked an ear and strained to listen, but all he heard was the heavy tick of the grandfather clock in the corner. House noises, he decided after a few moments. He walked over to the corner and looked at the enamelled face of the clock. It said ten o'clock. He glanced at his wrist and saw his watch was missing. He searched the pockets of his silk dressing gown, then realised he had left his watch upstairs in the bathroom. What was keeping Joan? She usually 'phoned promptly at nine-thirty every Saturday night. Lines busy, probably. He went back to his brandy.

The doorbell rang.

He threw back the remainder of the brandy and deposited the glass on the sideboard. He wasn't expecting anybody and he paused as his hand reached for the door handle. A messenger from Century House? Possibly.

One of the neighbours? Maybe. He opened the door and went out into the tiled hallway, and switched on the light. The wooden clogs he wore as slippers made hollow clicks against the tiles as he marched to the front door. When he got there, he called out. 'Who is it?' No reply. 'Answer me,' he said, his voice loud and authoritative. He turned quickly on his heels as he heard a noise behind him. His eyes opened wide in alarm. A tall man in jeans and a black sweater stood five yards away. He was pointing a gun. 'What the hell is going on? Who are you?' Cameron started to walk towards the man.

'Hold it,' warned Jackson, swinging his weapon from side to side. 'Stand still or you're a dead man.'

Cameron stopped in his tracks. A second man appeared through the doorway of the dining room. He too was armed. 'Who . . .? What : . .?' stammered Cameron as he tried to make sense of what was going on.

'Shut up,' said Jackson. The doorbell chimed again. 'Get the door.' Pavel stepped forward and menaced Cameron with his gun.

Cameron walked backwards until he came up against the door. He moved slowly, mechanically. He turned and released the door catch. Tawfiq charged in and grabbed him by the neck, forcing him up against the wall. Cameron's legs went weak. A machine pistol was shoved under his chin. He heard the American laugh at his fright and he slowly collapsed onto the cool tiles.

III

Pavel got back to the van first and threw open the back doors. In the darkening twilight he could make out the hunched and huddled figures of Tawfiq and Jackson as they half carried, half dragged, the inert form of Cameron down the driveway. Pavel stripped off his shoulder holster, and together with the MP5K, hung it up on a metal peg inside the van.

Cameron was in a state of mild shock, and Pavel h
given him a small dose of Nikethamide. He could no
take the chance of Cameron slipping into respiratory
shock. That would have ended the whole operation. He
could hear Jackson swearing and cursing with the effort
of carrying Cameron. Tawfiq laboured in silence, hardly
put out by the exertion. It was all going to plan.

'Here we go,' said Jackson. He let go of Cameron while
Tawfiq still held on. Cameron slipped onto his side and
opened his eyes. Jackson leant against the open door,
breathing heavily. Pavel bent down, and, with Tawfiq's
assistance, pulled Cameron to his feet. Cameron tried to
slump forward, but Pavel held him up and started to back
him into the rear of the van.

'Can you hear me, Mr Cameron?' asked Pavel. Weakly,
Cameron nodded his head. 'Good. Very good.' Tawfiq
produced the handcuffs. Pavel guided Cameron's arms
behind his back. Tawfiq snapped on the cuffs and then
climbed inside. Pavel and Jackson pushed from the front.
Finally, they got Cameron into the van. Tawfiq tied his
feet together and then Pavel climbed in beside him.
Jackson closed the doors.

Jackson went round to the front of the van. He threw
his MP5K and his shoulder holster onto the passenger
seat and swung into the driver's side. Headlights
suddenly blinded him, as a car came round the bend, a
blue light flashing from its roof. Jackson shielded his
eyes against the glare. 'Police,' he said. Tawfiq crawled
up behind him. Jackson could feel his breath on his neck.
It smelt foul. 'Stay put,' he whispered to Tawfiq.

The lights on the police car were dimmed. Jackson
edged his left hand over towards the machine pistol. He
gripped the butt and pulled it onto his knee. Tawfiq's
safety-catch clicked off. Jackson pushed open his door.
The passenger door of the police car opened and a uniformed officer started to get out. Jackson kept time with
him.

'Would you mind telling me what you're doing here?'

demanded Inspector Raison as he stood up and leant on the car door.

Jackson kept his left hand from view. He looked across to the driver whose face was suffused in a red glow from the car's instrument panel. Jackson saw him lean forward. He brought a microphone to his lips. Raison walked round the open door, heading for the van. Jackson brought out his machine pistol and opened fire.

The first burst caught Raison in the chest and threw him backwards, head over heels. The driver of the police car gaped open-mouthed. Jackson's next burst separated the policeman's head from his body as the windscreen shattered into millions of tiny, pointed shards.

Jackson dashed over to the car. He checked that both men were dead before getting back inside the van. He started the engine and drove off without a word, crashing into the side of the police car in the confined space, and running over the bloody remains of Inspector Raison.

London, England

I

Walsh stormed into his office shaking water droplets from his hand. 'No bloody towels in the toilet again,' he shouted.

'Godalming nick's just been on. They've lost contact with their Inspector.' said Pigott.

'Get them back on,' said Walsh, and dried his hands on the side of his trousers. 'They find anything at the Earls Court address yet?'

'Clean as a whistle so far,' said Pigott dialling. 'But they're still looking.'

Walsh took the receiver from Pigott. 'Commander Walsh here. Who am I speaking to?' He listened for a moment then took the receiver from his ear and pointed it at Pigott. 'Raison went down to the house with just his driver. No back-up. No guns. Idiot. Now everyone's gone chasing down there. Too late by now. Here, Tom, take over.'

Walsh sat down behind his desk and watched Pigott finish the conversation with the excited constable from Godalming. Finally he hung up. 'They'll call us back as soon as they hear anything,' said Pigott.

'When will our team be there?' said Walsh.

'Ten, fifteen minutes, perhaps.'

'Good. Then perhaps we'll find out just what's going on at that house.'

II

'I don't think he'll be there,' said Mercer. 'Probably used Chiddingfold as their forward base. They'll stash him somewhere else.'

'Possibly,' said Walsh. 'We'll know in a few minutes.' He bit into his ham sandwich from the canteen and made a face. Mercer left his in its wrapper. 'Not bad,' said Walsh with his mouth full. But he left the remainder uneaten. 'Why do you think they went after Cameron?' Mercer shrugged his shoulders and looked away. 'I've had the Director on twice. He contacted Abbeydore. There's an SAS group on stand-by. Did you know that?'

'No,' replied Mercer.

'If there's anyone in the cottage, my orders are to send in the SAS.'

'You called the Alpha Red Alert?' said Mercer.

'Nothing else I could do. Standing Orders.' He drank his coffee. 'So. What do they want Cameron for.'

'None of your business,' said Mercer after a pause. 'Has Zarev said anything?'

Walsh shook his head. 'Not a word.' He glanced at Mercer and smiled. 'Professional interest, that's all.'

They were sitting in the room next to Walsh's which he had commandeered in order to speak to Mercer privately about the night's events. He had told Mercer all that had transpired, and now they were waiting to hear from the team at Chiddingfold. Sergeant Pigott entered the room and brought the bad news. 'Empty,' he said. 'Dixon reckons they only just missed them.'

'Okay, Tom,' said Walsh. He got to his feet. 'Let's go and have a chat with Zarev.' The three men left the room and walked along the corridor, and down the stairs to the floor below.

Zarev was being held in a windowless cubicle about ten feet square. He was seated on a wooden chair with his hands chained behind his back. Two uniformed police officers stood guard over him. Walsh dismissed them as soon as he entered, but even then, the room seemed overcrowded. 'On your feet,' barked Walsh at the prisoner. Mercer stood to one side, against the wall. 'Okay, Tom,' said Walsh. Zarev pushed himself to his feet.

Mercer noticed that Pigott was wearing a pair of heavy black brogues. He hadn't been wearing them when Mercer first arrived. Mercer was sure of that. Pigott's shoes scuffed the floor as he walked over to Zarev. He stopped short of the man and glared at him. Then without warning, like a footballer striking a dead ball, he swung his left foot into Zarev's groin. Zarev's own bulk prevented him from doubling up. He let out a high-pitched whine, like steam escaping from a kettle. His knees bent and his backside hit the wall behind. His face turned bright red, then sickly white. He collapsed onto his knees, and fell over onto his side, his legs and shoulders jerking involuntarily.

Pigott prodded the man's hands with the toe of his shoe, then drove the heel into one of the thumbs that was hard up against the floor. Zarev shrieked. Mercer saw for the first time that the room was sound-proofed, and he recalled the Old Man's words about adopting the methods of the enemy. He turned away from the spectacle as Pigott kicked Zarev in the ribs.

'The dirty end of the business,' said Walsh casually. 'The kind you lot never see.' He put a hand on Mercer's shoulder and turned him back to look at the groaning figure of Todor Zarev. 'Let's have another word with him, shall we?' He pulled Mercer forward.

Mercer forced himself to look down at Zarev. His mouth was open and his lips were covered in stringy globules of saliva. His eyes darted back and forth, as if trying to locate the direction of the next assault. Mercer could see fear in those eyes, the fear of the bully who has had his own way for too long and who is at last receiving just retribution.

Walsh dropped to his haunches in front of Zarev's face and put a hand on the bald pate. 'Well, well Todor.' He patted the head and grinned. 'What's it like to be on the receiving end? Painful, isn't it? My Sergeant here is a quiet man normally. But he hates people like you. Understand?' Walsh pulled Zarev's head two or three times so that it looked as if the man was nodding yes in response to Walsh's question. 'Good,' said Walsh. 'Now listen very carefully. I'm going to leave you alone with my Sergeant for an hour. Then when you get out of hospital in about six weeks' time, I'm going to take you on a sight-seeing tour of London. Special points of interest will be the Soviet Embassy and Highgate. Plus one or two other places.' Walsh stood up and rubbed his knees. He bent over Zarev this time. 'And certain people are going to start asking why Todor Zarev hasn't been in touch for such a long time. And why he's driving round London with the Special Branch. And when some of those people asking the questions find themselves getting expelled, others will start putting two and two together. Get the picture?'

Zarev's eyes were steady now. But they were still frightened. Walsh began to walk slowly round the room. 'Then we'll put you away in a nice secluded country house. Only the security won't be so good, and the location will soon become common knowledge.' He stopped in his tracks. 'Still with me? Yes, I can see you are. It won't be very pleasant for you. You'll be shitting yourself, won't you? You'll know that one day, sooner or later, one of your pals, maybe even one who you trained yourself, is going to come creeping up on you. I don't think it'll be as simple as a single shot in the back of the neck, though.' Walsh rubbed his chin with his right hand. 'Ice-pick in the head?' He shook his head. 'Poison? A small ball placed just under the skin? Coated with Ricin. A slow and painful death. Ask Georgi Markov.' He went and stood over Zarev again. 'But then you can't, can you?'

Zarev tried to speak. Walsh dropped to his knees, and placed an ear close to the man's mouth. Mercer could hear the whispers but could not make them out. After a few minutes, Walsh got to his feet. 'Thank you, Todor.' He looked across at Pigott. 'Get him a doctor. Look after him.' He turned on his heels. 'Let's go,' he said to Mercer over his shoulder, and strode from the room.

III

'And not just the line to the cottage. I want all the lines in and around the village cut,' said Mercer. 'And get hold of Signals. I want a van with a carrier on it. Fifteen watts should be enough to block out any radio transmissions. Anyway, Signals should know what's what.' He put the phone down.

Walsh looked at him quizzically. 'What's that for?'

'They might have a radio as a back-up just in case they can't get through by 'phone.'

Walsh considered that for a moment. 'So they hope to sweat something out of Cameron. Is that it? Then relay it to the Soviet Embassy?'

'As I said before, it's none of your business. Your job is to get Cameron back. In one piece if possible.' Mercer couldn't look Walsh in the face.

'Not my job anymore. The SAS have moved in. I'll be there as an observer only. As will you.'

'The car's ready, sir,' said a policeman from the doorway.

'You finished?' asked Walsh.

'Yes. There's nothing else I can do here. Come on then.' said Mercer, happy to be getting out of the place. Zarev had wet his pants. The smell was still in Mercer's nostrils.

Worplesdon, England

I

'His head. Mind his head,' said Pavel sternly.

'What the fuck did you give him back there in the van?' asked Jackson.

'The Nikethamide worked too well,' said Pavel. 'He started to get excited. I had to sedate him with sodium amytal.'

'Well, he's knocked out now,' retorted Jackson. Pavel stood at the foot of the stairs supervising the operation. Tawfiq had hold of Cameron's feet, Jackson his head. They were halfway up the stairs, and Pavel could see that Jackson was getting more and more irritated as he struggled up backwards, trying to keep hold of Cameron. Pavel suspected that Cameron was shamming. He had only given him a tiny dose of sodium amytal, just enough to relax him, certainly not enough to cause this kind of effect. Cameron appeared to be totally unconscious.

Up they went, a stair at a time. Pavel was getting worried. Cameron had slept for most of the journey to Worplesdon, and they had arrived in the vicinity of the cottage more or less on schedule, and without any further contact with the police. But Zarev's car was not parked at the end of the lane. That had been the pre-arranged signal that it was safe to continue up to the house. Jackson had driven past and parked about a mile down the road. Then Jackson and Tawfiq had gone back to the cottage to see if there was anything wrong. While they were gone, Cameron had come to and started to struggle and shout. Pavel had had no option but to gag and sedate him.

He had chosen the amytal because it induced not only sedation, but also a mild hypnotic effect. He had already decided to use the sodium thiopentone on Cameron to extract from him the name of *Cedar*: the amytal would assist that drug in producing the effect Pavel wanted, a shallow, hypnotic sleep. He had a more powerful truth drug in reserve. Scopolomine, that induced twilight sleep. It was a favourite of the KGB, which they used indiscriminately in order to obtain confessions. But it was a most dangerous drug, and Pavel would only use it if and when the Thiopentone failed.

Jackson had his foot on the top step. 'Push,' he shouted at Tawfiq. Pavel noticed that Tawfiq was calm. He would have guessed that Tawfiq would have been the first to show signs of nerves and that Jackson would have remained cool and calm. In fact, it was the opposite. Jackson was nervy. And it had nothing to do with the deaths of the two policemen. He had been showing temperament before that, ever since they had arrived at Chiddingfold. Did he suspect? wondered Pavel.

Tawfiq tucked Cameron's legs under his arms and lifted them clear of the top stair. Pavel ran up the stairs, black doctor's bag in his hand. They were just laying Cameron on the bed when he entered the back bedroom.

It was a tiny room, with just enough space for a single bed and a small dresser which held a bowl and a water jug. The wallpaper was old and faded, and the flower print was lost in places, masked under rubbed-in grime and grease. There was no shade for the single, central light, which filled the room with a dull yellow glow, and turned all the corners into darkened recesses. There was a smell of dampness and mouldy plaster, and Pavel could see flecks of ceiling paint on the bare wooden floor. Heavy curtains kept the light inside.

'Give me the key,' said Jackson. Tawfiq handed it over. Jackson uncuffed one of Cameron's wrists, then looped the empty cuff round one of the uprights in the brass bedstead. Cameron suddenly sat up and made a grab for Jackson's throat just as he was about to snap the handcuff closed. Jackson dropped his head quickly, breaking

Cameron's tentative hold, and drove it into Cameron's stomach. At the same time, Tawfiq threw himself across Cameron's legs. 'Don't hurt him,' screamed Pavel, and dived at Jackson's back. Jackson shugged him off as he stood upright. Cameron lay groaning on the bed, holding his abdomen. 'Is he going to be ill?' asked Pavel, pushing past Jackson. 'Turn him on his side. I don't want him swallowing his vomit.'

'Leave him. He's alright,' snarled Jackson. 'Hold his left arm.' Pavel did as he was told, while Jackson finally managed to snap the handcuff shut. Tawfiq turned his attention to Cameron's ankles which he tied to the bottom of the bed with two pieces of stout cord. When they finished, Cameron was ready for Pavel.

'Cut the sleeve away,' Pavel told Jackson. Pavel opened the bag on the floor and took out two lengths of cord, similar to that which held Cameron's ankles. He passed one to Jackson when he had finished exposing the arm. 'Tie his wrist to the side of the bed. Elbow downwards.' Pavel watched the expert way in which Jackson tied the knots. Cameron's eyes were now closed, and his lips were pressed firmly together. 'Now this one. Just above the elbow. Tight, so that the veins stand out.'

Pavel went back to his bag and took out a hypodermic syringe and a small bottle of colourless liquid, sealed at the top with silver foil. He checked all Cameron's bonds, then sat down on the edge of the bed. 'You can go downstairs now,' he told Jackson and Tawfiq.

II

Jackson sat in the tiny kitchen next to the cooker eating a sandwich. He held his Beretta in his right hand. They had lost an hour when he and Tawfiq had had to reconnoitre the house when they found Zarev's car was not where it was supposed to be. He didn't like that. Something had gone wrong. Something had happened to

Zarev, otherwise he would be there with them. He had to admit he was scared. This operation wasn't like his usual run-of-the-mill assassinations. It was a lot more involved. And there were too many people to worry about. Particularly Tawfiq.

Zarev had taken Jackson aside after the briefing in the London flat and had told him that one of his jobs would be to kill Tawfiq when Pavel gave the word. He had agreed to do that, but it worried him. Was Zarev then planning to kill him? He realised that Zarev could be outside now, waiting to strike as soon as Jackson had taken care of Tawfiq. And had Tawfiq also been told that his task was to take care of Jackson? To Jackson, it looked as if the operation was one of those in which there would be only one survivor. And that would probably be Zarev. Cameron was already a dead man. Maybe Tawfiq was under orders to kill Pavel. Yes, he thought. Then he would kill Tawfiq, leaving Zarev to kill him. Bastards. Or . . . The combinations of killer and counter-killer whirled around his tired mind again. He gave up and finished eating. He told himself that he had to keep everyone in sight from now on. Nobody was going to get the drop on him.

III

Tawfiq was in the front room. He had brought his chair up to the window by the side of the front entrance, angling it so he could watch the path, while at the same time keep an eye on the kitchen door. He didn't want Jackson creeping up on him. Tawfiq was no fool. He knew all about Zarev from his training; knew that he was a killer; guessed that Zarev's main task was to see that no one survived. Tawfiq suspected he was outside, hiding, waiting to strike. But Tawfiq would be ready for him. But first he would take care of Jackson. He hated him. Pavel? Only if he caused problems. He was, after all, a doctor, a learned man. And a Russian, an ally. But he had better not get in the way, thought Tawfiq. He still had the war against Israel to fight, and no one was going to stop him from doing that.

IV

Mercer zipped up his fly and strolled back to the car.

'That was your boss on the blower,' said Walsh. 'Wants to speak to you.' Mercer shoved his hands into his jacket pocket and shivered. He was cold. He wished he'd had the foresight to bring along his overcoat. Walsh wore an old green anorak which he had found in the boot of the car. 'Are you going to?' For an answer Mercer walked away.

He went to the edge of the copse. On the other side was the cottage. Walsh joined him. 'What time is dawn?' asked Mercer. Walsh stepped back and looked at his watch. 'In about half an hour. Do you want to go and take a look?'

Mercer shook his head. 'Where are your men?'

'Here and there. Keeping out of trouble.'

'And the death and glory boys?'

'That I can't tell you. Somewhere within the fifty yard radius they marked off round the house. My team were told to stay out of it for their own safety. Know what I mean?' said Walsh.

'Got any more coffee?'

'There's some left in one of the flasks.'

V

Pavel mopped Cameron's brow with the cloth that was now heavy with sweat. Cameron's forehead glistened and his face was flushed a bright red. 'Mr Cameron. Mr Cameron. Tell me the name of the agent you know as *Cedar*. His real name. His Russian name.'

'No . . . No . . . Nobody . . . Nobody . . .'

Pavel was not getting anywhere. Cameron gave the same answer over and over again. The syringe of Thiopentone was almost empty. He would have to try Scopolomine. But could Cameron take it? He felt his pulse. It was fast. He got off the bed and went over to the dresser. He rinsed the cloth in the bowl then dropped it into the fresh water in the jug. He squeezed it out, but left it wet. He placed the soggy cloth on Cameron's face and gently washed it. He felt for the pulse again. It had slowed.

He withdrew the hypodermic from Cameron's forearm and threw it to one side. He got a fresh one from his bag, together with the phial of Scopolomine. He needed the answer from Cameron. They were all depending on him. They would all be up at the Embassy, ready for his call. Chebrikov would be waiting in Moscow Centre for the coded message from London. And the Premier? He would be there too, next to Chebrikov.

He stripped off the foil from the top of the bottle and inserted the needle. It had to work.

VI

Tawfiq stood in the doorway of the kitchen. Jackson was on his feet reaching for his MP5K. 'Did you hear it also?' asked Tawfiq.

'Yeah. Sounded like a car door slamming.' Jackson peered out of the kitchen window through the break in the curtains. 'Couldn't say what direction though.'

'Zarev?'

'Doubt it. You wouldn't hear him until he was on top of you. Get back to the front room. Keep your eyes and ears peeled,' ordered Jackson. As Tawfiq left, Jackson turned off the kitchen light. 'What's holding up that bloody doctor?'

VII

'They'll be going in about now,' said Mercer con-versationally. He was looking up at the sky. It reminded him of a black umbrella, dark directly overhead, but lighter at the edges. The sun was creeping up, scattering its power as grey and blue streaks against the night.

'Will you be alright on your own?' asked Walsh. 'I'm going forward to see Pigott.'

'Fine. Don't worry about me.'

'Are you armed?' Mercer said no. 'You can have this if you want.' Walsh pulled his Smith and Wesson out of his pocket and offered it to Mercer.

'No thanks. Safer without it.'

VIII

Tawfiq had pulled his chair closer to the window. Although it meant that he couldn't keep an eye on the kitchen doorway he consoled himself with the fact that Jackson would probably be doing what he was doing, staring out into the night, watching for any signs or sounds of approach. He also doubted whether Jackson could creep up on him without making a sound.

Dawn was coming. A word leapt into his mind. Salat. The time for prayer, for making obeisance to Almighty God, in the direction of Mecca. It was a long time since he had bowed his head in prayer. A shadow moved across his vision. He started to rise from his seat. The window pane suddenly looked like a gigantic spider's web centred on three tiny holes. As Tawfiq was thrown backwards over his chair, he heard the crisp, precise shots, and felt the hot, sticky blood run into his eyes. He was dead before he touched the ground.

IX

Jackson had seen something moving. He ducked down below the level of the window onto all fours and scrambled through the front room to confer with Tawfiq. He arrived just as Tawfiq's body completed its somersault over the chair. Jackson came to a halt on his knees and at the same time sent a burst of automatic fire through the broken window. The glass shattered and crashed to the floor. He swung round, resting the gun on his hip, and fired into the front door. Wood splinters flew in all directions. He got to his feet and dashed to the foot of the stairs. He felt something sting in his left shoulder, and then he was running, shouting, climbing upwards, looking for Pavel, unaware of the explosion above.

X

Pavel was stretched out on the bed in the front bedroom.

The first thing he heard was the sound of broken glass, quickly followed by a series of rapid shots. Then a great ball of light lit up the back room where Cameron's body lay. He was deafened by the loud explosion which he felt rather than heard, and his whole body shook, as did the rickety bed. He forced himself to roll off the bed and he scrambled to his feet.

He felt groggy and his eyes were watering. He staggered to the open door in time to see Jackson at the top of the stairs. Jackson's mouth was moving and the muscles of his jaw were set firm and rigid. Blood was coming from a shoulder wound. He was shouting at Pavel, but Pavel could not hear him. A man dressed all in black, bent into a crouch, hopped out of the back room. He shot Jackson five times in the chest, as Jackson was still wildly gesturing and mouthing to Pavel.

As if in slow motion, Pavel drew his own weapon and

shot the intruder before he could swing round. Pavel saw Jackson fall backwards down the stairs. His killer rolled forwards and fell at Pavel's feet. Pavel stepped over him. The man had no face. It was covered in a black ski-mask. Pavel stooped and pulled off the mask. He put it on and went downstairs.

About half-way down, he found his hearing was coming back. The sound of his own gunshots was ringing in his ears. As he reached Jackson's body, a figure appeared at the foot of the stairs, dressed all in black, like the man he had just killed. The figure hesitated for a fraction of a second, and started to lower his gun. Pavel shot him just as the realisation dawned that here was the enemy, as he tried to correct his mistake and bring his weapon to bear again.

Pavel peered into the room. It was empty except for Tawfiq's body. But Pavel heard a noise in the kitchen. He made a dash for the shattered window, leapt onto the sill, and dived through head first. He curled his body and rolled as he hit the grass. It was damp and dew-covered. He kept low to the ground, remembering his training from the two-week refresher course, and headed for the copse that faced the cottage.

XI

Mercer had heard the shots and the explosion. He thought he had seen the flash of the concussion grenade above the trees, but he could not be sure. He walked to the edge of the copse again, and stopped, uncertain whether to proceed any further. He decided to stay where he was. Walsh would bring him the news, good or bad.

He had to admit to himself that he couldn't care less about the outcome. He hoped that Cameron would come out of it alive. But if he didn't, then Mercer was not going to lose any sleep over it. Besides not liking the man, he couldn't help thinking that Cameron had brought it all upon himself. Cameron had lied about *Cedar* and their meetings together. Mercer had proof of that. As to why Cameron lied, Mercer couldn't say. But he was determined to find out. It would have to come out in the inquiry that would follow the night's events. Fordyce couldn't keep it quiet. Mercer would demand an explanation.

He turned his back on the wood and started to walk back to the car. A lot of people had died since *Cedar* first came on the scene. Mercer just hoped that whoever he was, he was still safe and secure, and that he would be able to supply the Service with intelligence, even though it would not be coming directly from the Politburo as Cameron had said. Otherwise, the dead, particularly those from the networks, would have died in vain.

'Stop,' said Pavel in a harsh whisper. Mercer froze to the spot. 'Turn around slowly.' Mercer did as he was told. 'Keep your hands where I can see them.'

Mercer looked at the barrel of the gun pointing straight at his chest, and then at the man. He wore jeans that were torn and streaked with dirt, topped by a black sweater. He held a ski-mask loosely by his side. He was tall and thin and his features and skin colour were European. His English had no trace of an American accent, so Mercer concluded that the man was the Russian, Pavel. Details of the kidnappers had been relayed to Mercer and Walsh as they motored down to the cottage. Zarev had been most helpful after his encounter with Sergeant Pigott. 'Dr Pavel Yosipovich Patukhov?' said Mercer.

Pavel's lips and eyes showed a trace of amusement. 'Mr Mercer,' he replied. Mercer could see he was tense, though he did not appear to be nervous. His hand holding the gun was steady. Only his mouth moved. 'Back up to the car,' he ordered. Mercer began to step backwards. Pavel followed, keeping his distance. 'Keep going,' warned Pavel as Mercer faltered in the long grass. 'That'll do.' Mercer glanced sideways and saw the bonnet of the car. 'Over that way.' Pavel waved his pistol in the direction of the car boot. Mercer obeyed.

'I haven't got the keys,' said Mercer.

Pavel shook his head. 'No matter. The car-phone is all I need.' He looked into the passenger window while trying to keep Mercer in view.

'What did you use on Cameron? Drugs or Drudgery?' Pavel ignored the questions and pulled open the door. 'I assume he talked?'

'Under Scopolomine? Who wouldn't?' said Pavel.

'So you know all about *Cedar*?' said Mercer. He had to play for time, in the hope that Walsh or some of the SAS would come to his rescue.

Pavel motioned Mercer forward. 'The door,' he said. Mercer stepped forward. 'There's nothing to know about *Cedar*. Nothing. Nothing at all.' Mercer froze in his tracks, his mind racing. Pavel laughed loudly and Mercer could see the tension drain from his body. 'The door. Open it.'

Mercer launched himself at Pavel. Pavel jumped back, and Mercer fell flat on his face. He heard the gun click on an empty chamber. He looked up. Pavel pulled the trigger again. Click! The magazine was empty. Mercer got to his feet, his whole body shaking. Pavel patted his pockets frantically, searching for another magazine.

Mercer moved towards him. Pavel gripped the barrel of his gun and stood his ground. It did not make a very effective club, but he brandished it at Mercer who retreated to the open passenger door. 'Move away,' said Pavel fiercely. 'I will kill you if I have to.' Mercer's mouth was dry. He spread his arms wide and braced his body against the car. He brought his right leg back, preparing to kick out when Pavel came in range. 'They will find out sooner or later about your conspiracy. So why risk death just to delay the inevitable?'

'Wait,' said Mercer as Pavel started to move in. Over Pavel's shoulder, Mercer could see two men in black racing towards them from the copse. 'It's too late.' He pointed past Pavel. 'The police are coming.' Pavel's eyes followed the pointing finger. He looked back at Mercer.

'They will kill you if you don't drop your gun.' Mercer put out his hand. 'Give it to me,' he said, approaching Pavel.

Pavel raised his left arm, the fist clenched so that the knuckles showed white, then let it drop to his side. The Beretta slipped from his hand to the ground. He sagged his head in defeat. Mercer went and stood by his side. He waved on the two SAS men.

The troopers slowed down as they saw Mercer and Pavel side by side. But when they got to within a few yards of them, the man to Mercer's left suddenly broke into a sprint and dived into Mercer, his shoulder striking him in the midriff. As Mercer was knocked off his feet, he saw the second SAS man run up to Pavel and shoot him twice in the head. Pavel staggered and fell, his head a bloody pulp, and crashed into the car, coming to rest against the front wing.

Mercer gripped his winded stomach with one hand, while he tried to brush the spray of blood from his face with the other. 'Why did you do that?' he screamed. 'Why? Why?' He reached out to the rear bumper and tried to pull himself upright. The SAS men did not give him a second glance. 'Why did you kill him?' he roared hysterically. He slipped over on the wet grass. The soldiers had hold of Pavel now, one to each arm, and were dragging the body back the way they had come, back into the woods, like two animals securing their victim from greedy, prying competitors.

Mercer finally managed to get to his feet. He bent double and retched. There was blood on his shoes, his jacket, and the front end of the car. 'Bastards,' he shouted, and was sick again. The SAS men were almost at the copse. Mercer could see three other black clad figures waiting to greet them. 'Why did you have to kill him?' he whispered. There were tears of pain and anger in his eyes.

London, England

I

Mercer stood on the pavement. Walsh scrambled across the back seat to close the door.

'I didn't know, Joe. Believe me.'

'It doesn't matter.' Mercer shuffled his feet and turned to look at the front of the house. 'Whose is this place?'

Walsh shrugged. 'Belongs to Sir James Ffitch-Heyes.' He ducked back into the car. 'See you,' he said as he slammed the door closed. Mercer saw him speak to the driver and the car roared off into the traffic. The sun was shining strongly and it promised to be another hot day. Mercer felt cold.

He walked up the short flight of scrubbed steps and rang the bell. A uniformed butler answered the door. Mercer started to enter but the man blocked his way. He caught sight of the tip of his left shoe perched on the top step: it was scuffed and muddied; the other matched. His trousers, particularly around the knees, were damp and dirty. His hands and jacket were streaked with mud, and his shirt collar was stiff with splashes of blood. He looked and felt a mess. 'Mercer,' he said to the butler. The man tutted and stepped back to allow Mercer to enter, reluctance and distaste showing clearly in his features.

He made Mercer wipe his feet on a large coconut mat just inside the vestibule, standing over him like an angry parent with a naughty child. He handed Mercer a clothes brush, but he declined to use it. The butler recovered quickly, then led Mercer along a carpeted corridor to a room at the back of the house, which he guessed would be the morning room in this part of Kensington. 'A Mr Mercer,' announced the butler, before withdrawing.

Fordyce sat in an armchair by the window, reading a

sheaf of papers. Sir Peter Ralston stood at the drinks cabinet pouring himself a brandy. 'I'll have one too,' said Fordyce. He looked up and smiled. 'And I'm sure Joseph will join us.'

II

'*Cedar* was a figment of Cameron's imagination,' said Mercer.

'Really. Is that what the Russian doctor told you?' asked Fordyce.

'He confirmed my suspicion. I'd suspected something of the kind for some time.'

'Clever you,' said Fordyce. He glanced over to the Old Man who had taken a seat in the corner. Mercer watched the exchange. The Old Man looked well; he had lost a lot of weight and he seemed to radiate good health. His face and hands were tanned, and his hair, cut close to the head, was bleached white. His dark blue suit fitted him snugly. He looked like a prosperous City broker. He had barely acknowledged Mercer's greeting and was prepared to let Fordyce do all the talking. He nodded to Fordyce as he brought his drink to his lips.

Mercer slumped back into the seat. He was tired. Images from the morning's events played themselves back in his mind, and occasionally he found them intruding on his consciousness as he tried to concentrate on what he was saying, and what he heard in reply. 'They used Scopolomine on him. He told them all about *Cedar*. Nothing. *Cedar* doesn't exist.'

'But Moscow Centre still believe he exists and that is the important thing'. Fordyce smiled at Mercer. 'What is more, they must continue to believe in his existence until the SALT talks are concluded.'

III

'. . . But if the Americans know the Russians want to talk disarmament, why aren't they prepared to listen?' asked Mercer.

'You said it all in your original assessment to the JIC,' said Fordyce smugly. 'Russia is broke. She can't afford to compete any longer in the arms race. The country is falling apart at the seams. Corruption is rife. The people are disgruntled and disillusioned. Alcoholism is soaring. The crime rate. . . '

'All the more reason to try to reach an agreement with them.'

Fordyce shook his head slowly, his eyes closed. 'You have it the wrong way round.' He finished his drink and held out his glass. 'Refill, Peter, please.' The Old Man stepped forward and took the glass. Mercer watched him at the drinks cabinet. Mercer had checked up on Airwork Industries and its dynamic chairman, Sir James Ffitch-Heyes. He supposed it was inevitable, really. Nothing was as it seemed. Everything, everybody, changed. He was the odd man out, the one who had refused to move, to adapt. The feeling had come over him the moment he had set eyes on the Old Man in the company of Fordyce. That was why he had not exploded in anger when he had entered the room, but had determined to sit it out, to listen and try to see what was behind it all. Perhaps, he told himself, he had something to learn. 'Cheers,' said Fordyce as his drink arrived.

'Now, Joseph,' continued Fordyce. 'Think about it. What if Russia and the West come to an agreement at the next round of SALT talks in the autumn? Stockpiles reduced. Missiles pulled back and destroyed. Research and development halted. Disarmament. Every peace-group's dream. Peace at last.'

'Fine by me. By everybody, I should imagine.'

Fordyce raised his eyebrows and cocked his head to one

side. 'But how long do you think the peace would last?'

'With the proper supervision and . . .'

'No. No,' interrupted Fordyce. 'That is all understood. What would a disarmament agreement do for the Russians?'

Mercer began to see what Fordyce was driving at but he wanted to hear it from him. 'You tell me. You seem to know it all.' Mercer sat back in his seat, his brandy untouched.

'Simple,' said Fordyce smugly. 'A disarmament agreement would provide the Russians with the luxury of both time and money to put their house in order. Once the Premier has consolidated his power, he will take Mother Russia by the scruff of the neck and shake her until all the rottenness falls out. It may take him five or ten years. But he will succeed. He will sort it out and solve all her domestic problems, build up her economy, her industrial might, her agricultural base.'

'And leave the West with no market for its excess grain?' said Mercer cynically.

'That certainly is a consideration in our overall strategy. A small one, but an important one nevertheless.' The Old Man's voice came from the back of the room. Mercer turned to stare at him, but he looked away.

'Thank you, Peter,' said Fordyce with a wave of his hand. 'Peace can only benefit the Soviet Union. It would be a disaster for the West.'

'No more profitable defence contracts for the arms industry? They would probably go broke,' said Mercer. 'Another small consideration, no doubt, in the strategy?' He could feel the Old Man's eyes on him.

Fordyce did not rise to the bait. He continued unabashed. 'Peace will reign throughout the world while the Kremlin is rebuilding the Soviet State. But what happens when it is all done, when Russia is strong and vital? Will she continue to honour the agreements, the treaties?'

'Why not?' asked Mercer. 'People can get used to peace' just as they can to war.'

'Not the Soviets. Their ultimate goal is world domination. Always was, always will be. The truth is that the Kremlin would break *any* agreement between East and West whenever they thought it would be propitious, whenever they felt strong enough to do so. The West would be jeopardising its own future by coming to any disarmament agreement with the Russians.

'What you're saying is that we cannot afford peace with the Soviets?'

'Indeed I am. Our present strategy is based on certain computer predictions. Russia's resources are far greater than those of the West. Given time, the expertise and technology from the West, a stable and willing workforce, and Russia would become a giant of terrifying proportions. A far greater threat than she has ever been. And then it would be the Western Alliance which would be led a merry dance, which would be left behind in the arms race. We would have our backs to the wall, unable to afford the immense costs of holding parity with the Russians.' Fordyce was almost breathless by the time he finished speaking. His face was red with the effort, and he motioned the Old Man forward for another drink.

'Have it your own way.'

'Let me tell you what your strategy is,' said Mercer as he watched Fordyce recover. 'It involves keeping the pressure on Russia. Escalating the arms race. Turning the screw so that the Kremlin leadership cannot turn their attention, their financial resources, to the problems which I detailed in my original assessment. The aim is to keep the Russians in the arms race, however unwilling they may be to continue the spiral, in the hope that Russia will bankrupt herself and her society will collapse and disintegrate.'

'Exactly,' said Fordyce with a huge grin. 'We drive Russia to the wall and watch her fall apart.'

'The computers cannot be wrong,' said Mercer, with heavy sarcasm.

Fordyce pounded the arms of his chair. 'It is the only

option the West has. We will never be safe as long as communist Russia exists. We cannot risk a nuclear war with her. So, we push her to bankruptcy and social decay. Her own people, after all, have done most of the spade work.'

'And the Russians will never see through this strategy? Won't react to it? Mightn't they start a nuclear war knowing they are going under, that they have nothing to lose?'

'They would be too disadvantaged to fight. Too near collapse to do anything but surrender. That is the prediction.'

Mercer had the impression that Fordyce was reading from a prepared script. An image of Fordyce the android flashed before him. 'Do your predictions take into account that by the turn of the century the Muslim inhabitants of the Soviet Republics will number more than half the total Russian population? What if a latter-day Khomeini was to arise amongst them as the country was falling apart? He'd have tremendous fun if he ever laid hands on the Soviet nuclear arsenal. Wouldn't he? And those Muslim fundamentalists have no great love for the West.'

Fordyce shook his head. 'No. That is all irrelevant. We are very close to the realisation of our plans. Five years. Ten at the outside. And Russia will cease to exist as an effective force in the world.'

'That short a time?' Mercer looked unconvinced. 'And the West will then march into Russia and take over? Or a native government will arise that will be anti-communist and pro-Western?'

'Both are possibilities which the computers have forecasted.'

'Whose computers exactly?' asked Mercer. 'Airwork Industries? Those of Ffitch-Heyes' friends in the Ares Club?'

'That has nothing to do with it,' said Fordyce stiffly. He turned to the Old Man. 'Peter. Could you ask Cobbet to rustle up something to eat? A few sandwiches, perhaps?' The Old Man left the room.

Mercer waited until he had Fordyce's attention again. 'So you don't accept that the Premier's current peace overtures are genuine? Just Soviet disinformation.'

'Oh, they may well be real and well-intentioned. He has to be thinking about disarmament because of the parlous state of the Russian economy and the state of the country. But the Premier won't be there forever. In fact, he probably won't be alive by the end of the year. It's the next generation of Russian leaders that the strategy is aimed at. They will be the ones who will start the next round of the Cold War after Russia is back on her feet.'

Cobbet entered with a tray of sandwiches covered in silver foil, which he removed after placing them on the table. As he bent over to do so, Mercer noticed the butt of a gun protruding from inside the man's liveried jacket. He gave Mercer a hostile glare as he left. The Old Man did not return for a while, not until Mercer and Fordyce had made inroads into the mound of ham, beef and chicken sandwiches. Mercer was glad of the respite. His mind felt numb, and he needed time to collect his thoughts.

Fordyce offered another drink, but Mercer refused as his first was still untouched. 'It's after midday, you know,' quipped Fordyce as he helped himself to another brandy. The Old Man returned and took up his seat in the corner.

'Well then,' said Fordyce as he dusted bread crumbs from his fingers.

'Where does *Cedar* fit in to your strategy?' said Mercer.

'Right in the middle. The lynch pin. He is in the process of sabotaging the Russian peace initiative.'

'The Russians can't do a deal in Geneva with a traitor in the Kremlin?'

'Correct,' said Fordyce.

'They will be made to look intransigent, unwilling to talk peace. Their earlier initiatives will be seen as disinformation,' said the Old Man.

'The old war cry. Everything that the Russians do and

say is all part of their insidious plan to mislead the West,' said Mercer shaking his head.

'Of course. But you also have to remember that we in the West, unlike our Russian counterparts, have to justify our every move in the arms race. That's the price which democracy exacts.'

'And there's still some resistance to the sitings of *Cruise* and *Pershing* in Europe,' said Mercer. 'To quell that you have to make it look as if it is the Russians who are not ready and willing to talk peace so that Western public opinion will see the deployment simply as anticipation of Soviet truculence and their determination to maintain the Cold War.'

'Very good,' said Fordyce. '*Cedar* will ensure the talks collapse, and the Russian Military will be waiting on the sidelines with their hands out, to extract from the Premier the necessary resources that have so far been denied them.'

'The Soviets will be the warmongers. Not us. And you accuse them of disinformation,' said Mercer with a laugh.

'Joe,' said the Old Man. 'A lot of this depends on you.'

IV

Mercer got out of the police car at the front of his apartment building. The two uniformed police officers waited until he went in before driving off. He lived on the top floor, the sixth, but he took the lift to the fourth floor and knocked on the door of number eight. Hugh Sheaver answered. They knew each other casually, enough to exchange good mornings and weather reports whenever they met on the stairs, in the lobby or the elevator. Mercer explained that his telephone was out of order. Sheaver offered him the use of his. He called Todd. They agreed to meet later that night.

He walked upstairs to his floor. By the time he reached

it, his legs were aching. He leant against the door while he looked for his keys. The corridor was quiet. The flat opposite had been empty for some time, and Mercer liked it that way. The stillness suited him, and it gave him the feeling of isolation, of being cut off from the rest of the building's occupants, from the rest of the city.

He unlocked the door and went straight to the bathroom, where he tore off his clothes.

V

He had to get rid of the mud. The dirt. The smell. And the blood. The water was getting colder, but Mercer persisted. He scrubbed and rubbed his body, his face, his hair, lathering up the soap and spreading it all over himself before ducking under the cascading water. But he didn't feel clean. The shower water was ice-cold now and he began to shiver. He stayed put for another minute then turned off the tap and stepped out of the plastic cubicle. His dirty clothes lay in a heap in front of him and he kicked them aside as he went in search of a towel.

He found one in the bedroom and rubbed himself dry. He lay down naked on the bed and closed his eyes. He remembered the alarm clock. He reached over and set it for eleven o'clock. He was meeting Todd at midnight. One hour or so should be enough to shake off pursuers that Fordyce would undoubtedly have waiting for him outside, he thought. He tried to sleep. His stomach was upset and it gurgled its protests at him. He had eaten too many sandwiches, too quickly.

He drifted into a half-sleep. Cameron. The Old Man. Fordyce. Their faces loomed up in his dreams, laughing at him. They had all betrayed him, and used him. He waved his fist at them. He wasn't going to let them threaten him anymore.

VI

'You betrayed my networks,' accused Mercer. 'Five networks gone. There's only Solicitor in Kiev and Teacher in Vladivostock remaining.'

'Binder, actually,' said Fordyce.

Mercer shook his head. 'No. You did.' He pointed at Fordyce, then at the Old Man. 'And you.' He spat out the words. 'For the sake of some computer predictions.'

'For a strategy that will permanently remove the Russian threat from the face of the earth,' corrected Fordyce. 'Those men and women will not have died in vain.'

'They died. That's the important thing,' said Mercer sadly.

'The loss of your people to the KGB was essential,' said the Old Man. 'We could only have let the Soviets know that they had a traitor in the Politburo through Binder. He gave them your networks. It convinced Moscow Centre both of his loyalty and of the presence of *Cedar*.'

Mercer remembered the occasion when Tuert had briefed them on the loss of Doctor back in April. Binder had looked ill. Mercer now knew the reason why. He thought of Mary and how she would react to her brother's treachery.

Fordyce spoke. 'The KGB recruited Binder at university. He slipped into the Service in the bad old days of negative vetting. He was a deep penetration agent, not meant to surface until he was in a top position.'

'How was he blown?' asked Mercer.

'He came in himself. To Markfield. At the time of the Blunt exposè. Markfield put him on ice. Didn't tell anybody about it. As it turned out, he fitted neatly into the scheme of things.' Fordyce looked smug as he spoke. Mercer felt like punching him.

'Who's his control?'

'Your old friend, the KGB resident Arkady Guk. A Chebrikov man. He took the news of *Cedar* back to Chebrikov in person.'

'And he wasn't suspicious that Binder had broken cover, had surfaced before his time?' said Mercer.

'The importance of the information quelled any suspicions. In fact Binder received a message of congratulations from Chebrikov. Giving them your networks also helped.'

'Guk will smell a rat if Binder's not caught soon. So will Moscow Centre. The leak's too big, at too high a level'. He stared at Fordyce. 'But you know that don't you?' Mercer began to see where he fitted in, why Fordyce had taken the time to explain it all to him. The bottom line, as the Americans said, was about to be revealed.

Fordyce rubbed his hands together. 'Very true, Joseph.' He sat on the edge of his seat. The Old Man came to stand close by. 'We have various ways of dealing with that contingency.'

'Which one you choose will depend on me. Is that it?'

'We cannot force you to stay in the Service,' said Fordyce. 'And we cannot afford to let you leave. Not with what you know about *Cedar*.'

'Why don't you just remove me? Permanently. One more dead man shouldn't bother you too much.' Mercer gripped the arm rests. 'Why didn't you get the SAS to shoot me this morning while they were murdering the doctor?'

'We don't work that way,' said Fordyce sharply. 'You're one of us.'

'So were my people in Russia whom you betrayed,' shouted Mercer.

'Joe. Listen to me,' said the Old Man, interrupting. Fordyce looked indignant. 'What's done is done. You can't change that. But if you co-operate, you leave here a free man, free of the Service. Free to do whatever you like.'

'Co-operate with you.' The Old Man took a step backwards, his face turning white despite his tan, as he heard the venom in Mercer's voice.

'If you don't go along with us, you'll find yourself in prison for a very long time,' said Fordyce wagging a finger at Mercer.

Mercer laughed. There was a trace of hysteria in the laugh. He recognised it as such. 'God Almighty,' he said quietly.

'We can kill two birds with one stone,' said Fordyce angrily.

'How's that?' asked Mercer wearily. He rubbed his eyes. Flashes of light appeared before them, followed by a blackness illuminated with tiny spots of white.

'We could have you arrested as the mole. Show Guk that we have our traitor and allay any suspicions that may be forming.'

'Guk wouldn't go for that. He knows that Markfield would never make a mistake like that.'

'Don't be so sure, Joe,' said the Old Man.

'What would you use for evidence?'

'For example,' said Fordyce taking up the cudgel. 'Besides myself and Cameron, who is now dead, there is only yourself who knew about *Cedar* and had access to the identities of the Russian networks.'

'Binder also.'

'Guk knows that. But from our side, Binder didn't have access to the networks. You may have noticed that he steered well clear of your Section even though he was to take over from you in April. Officially, and Markfield knows this, Binder could not have been the mole.'

'Then there's your contact with Todd,' said the Old Man.

'What about it? You know . . .'

'What about it?' repeated Fordyce in amazement. 'We know what you told him. We've got all his papers.'

'It's like that, is it?' said Mercer.

'Does the International Cocoa Organisation mean anything to you? Of course it does.' Fordyce paused. 'Boris Sedov? Interpreter?' He looked at the Old Man.

'Sedov's a close friend of Todd's,' said the Old Man. 'He's also one of Guk's hoods. A good one.'

'We could put you away for twenty years,' said Fordyce in triumph.

'It wouldn't hold up in court. Circumstantial,' argued Mercer without much conviction.

'Don't be silly, Joe. You'd go down. You know it.' The Old Man came to stand over Mercer who had buried his face in his hands. 'You've been under a lot of pressure lately. You're upset now after this morning's events. Go home. Think about it. Come and see me and we'll talk.'

Mercer raised his head. 'Not to you,' he said.

'We don't want you talking out of school. We know that you have been insdiscreet with Todd on one or two occasions. We don't want a repeat. There's too much at stake,' warned Fordyce.

The Old Man continued. 'We just want your silence. There are other ways of ensuring Guk retains his faith in Binder. But unless you agree to keep quiet, we will use you to do that. We'll lock you up. Think about it.' He put a hand on Mercer's shoulder. He shrugged it off.

'There was no heart attack, was there?' whispered Mercer. The Old Man shook his head. 'And the Falklands? Was the information withheld from you so that the Peterhouse Mafia could show you as incompetent?'

Again the Old Man shook his head. 'No, it wasn't. You shouldn't have told Todd that, you know.'

'You told me. I believed you. Why did you lie to me, your friend?'

'It was Tommy Conway in Buenos Aires. He wasn't up to it. The Argentinians had him stitched up with a couple of women and plenty of booze.' He reached out to touch Mercer again, but he sank back into his chair. 'But they blamed me. They were going to throw me out on the scrap heap.'

'So you sold out. Gave in to them. For the job with the men with the money. Betrayed me. Yourself. Your own people.'

'No. I didn't. I just saw the sense of their arguments. What they were trying to achieve.'

'You saw what you wanted to see because they had you tied down. Now all you can see is bloody computers and their predictions. And you let people die because of what those predictions say.'

Fordyce got to his feet. 'Those predictions which you obviously scorn have been correct so far. Everything is going to schedule. You'll see. The Russians are beaten.'

'If your bloody computers are so good, how come they didn't forecast the attack on Cameron as one of the options open to the Russians?' Both men looked at Mercer in surprise.

VII

He left all the lights on in the flat. He did not want to signal to his pursuers that he was on his way out. He closed and locked the door. He went to the lift shaft and pressed the button. He would go down to the second floor and make his way out of the caretaker's door. They would probably have it covered, but there were three different directions he could take, and he knew he could lose them somewhere along the alleyways that ran behind the buildings.

He would tell Todd everything. Maybe Todd would take it no further. That was up to him to decide. Mercer just had to get it all off his chest. Todd would appreciate learning that he, too, was under observation. And had been for some considerable time. Fordyce and his mob had planned it all down to the last detail. But he wasn't worried about the consequences. They could arrest him. Put him on trial. But he would have his day. They couldn't shut him up. He wasn't going to be threatened by Fordyce again. He had given in to them over staying on in the Service when he had wanted to leave, and later over the revision of his assessment. But not now. Maybe if he had stood his ground on that first occasion, he would not be in this predicament now. He should have seen it all coming.

The light by the elevator door told him the lift was on its way. If they put him on trial, he definitely would tell all. Todd would help. He would get it published. And the *Cedar* scheme would fall to pieces. Perhaps there might even be a disarmament agreement reached in Geneva after all.

He felt pleased at the prospect. The lift was almost there. They wouldn't risk a trial, he told himself. They couldn't hope to keep him quiet. The doors opened with a rush of air.

As Mercer stepped into the void, as his body was battered back and forth against the sides of the rectangular shaft that dropped seven floors to the basement, he realised that they couldn't risk a trial, had no intention of ever doing so. They had incriminated him to such an extent, that his body, broken and bloodied, would be all that they needed. They had the proof, the evidence of Mercer's treachery. They wouldn't want anyone to question it. And Guk would be pleased that the Service had the wrong man. He and Binder could look forward to a much longer, fruitful relationship. As his body struck the unresisting basement floor, his last thought was whether Sheaver knew his 'phone was bugged.

VIII

Mercer's death received a short paragraph on page six of the evening newspaper. It was two lines longer than the report on page seven which told of the death at Victoria Station of Thomas Todd, a freelance newspaper reporter who died beneath the wheels of a train. Police were investigating both deaths.

EPILOGUE – JUNE 1986

To date, no agreement between East and West on arms control and disarmament has been reached.

About nine months after Mercer's death, in the spring of 1986, America detonated three nuclear devices in the Nevada Desert as part of the continuing Star Wars programme. A week later, Pravda, reflecting official Soviet policy, called on the Soviet Goverment to maintain its self-imposed moratorium on nuclear testing. In the same edition, Pravda forecast a bumper grain and cereal harvest for the Soviet Union, indicating that imports from the West would not be necessary.

In the early hours of Tuesday 15th April, American FI–II fighter bombers of the 20th Tactical Fighter Wing, from two bases inside England, and augmented by carrier-based aircraft of the US Sixth Fleet, carried out raids against selected targets inside Libya.

At the same time, four Cruise missile launchers, heavily guarded by American servicemen, were deployed at West Down Plantation on Salisbury Plain. In West Germany, at Ulm and Mutlangen, *Pershing* missiles were brought onto their launching pads. *Cruise* missiles were also deployed at Comiso in Italy.

These missile movements and the build-up to the Libyan raid, were all classed as routine NATO exercises. There can be no doubt that the missile deployments were an insurance against possible retaliation by the Soviet Union for the American attack on her ally, Libya.

The Russian response to the bombing raid and the threat from the missiles was to inform the West that peace talks were still possible.

During the weekend of 26–27th April, 1986, an accident occurred in a RBMK 1000 nuclear reactor in the Chernobyl nuclear power plant, 80 miles north of Kiev. A radioactive cloud was released into the atmosphere which was blown across Russia and into northern Europe and Scandinavia, causing widespread and deadly pollution.

Within a radius of 20 miles of the Chernobyl site, habitation will not be possible for many years. Beyond that, hundreds of thousands of hectares of arable land will retain radioactive contaminants for hundreds, if not thousands of years. Cultivation of the land will be impossible. Kiev is the capital of the Soviet Republic of the Ukraine. The Ukraine is Russia's bread basket. There will be no harvest this year, or in the foreseeable future. Grain exports from America to Russia will re-commence in the autumn, thereby stabilising the Western agricultural economy and further stretching Russian resources.

BETWEEN THE BALANCE OF POWER AND GLOBAL
CHAOS, ONE MAN WALKED THE KNIFE EDGE . . .

THE MAN WHO WAS SATURDAY

DEREK LAMBERT

Moscow treated defectors from the West with kid-gloves. That is, until
they had outlived their usefulness. But the American Calder was different.
He had defected to Russia with information so explosive that even the
iron-clad regime of the Kremlin shook with fear. It had kept him alive. Until
now. For Calder is desperately keen to return to the West . . .

So they place the ruthless and scheming Spandarian on his trail, a KGB
chief with a mind as sharp as the cold steel of an ice pick. And as back-up
they unleash Tokarev, a professional assassin who kills for pleasure . . .

0 7221 5374 0   ADVENTURE THRILLER   £2.95

Also by Derek Lambert in Sphere Books:
TRANCE
I, SAID THE SPY
THE RED DOVE
THE JUDAS CODE
THE GOLDEN EXPRESS

A selection of bestsellers from Sphere

FICTION

WANDERLUST	Danielle Steel	£3.50 ☐
LADY OF HAY	Barbara Erskine	£3.95 ☐
BIRTHRIGHT	Joseph Amiel	£3.50 ☐
THE SECRETS OF HARRY BRIGHT	Joseph Wambaugh	£2.95 ☐
CYCLOPS	Clive Cussler	£3.50 ☐

FILM AND TV TIE-IN

INTIMATE CONTACT	Jacqueline Osborne	£2.50 ☐
BEST OF BRITISH	Maurice Sellar	£8.95 ☐
SEX WITH PAULA YATES	Paula Yates	£2.95 ☐
RAW DEAL	Walter Wager	£2.50 ☐

NON-FICTION

AS TIME GOES BY: THE LIFE OF INGRID BERGMAN	Laurence Leamer	£3.95 ☐
BOTHAM	Don Mosey	£3.50 ☐
SOLDIERS	John Keegan & Richard Holmes	£5.95 ☐
URI GELLER'S FORTUNE SECRETS	Uri Geller	£2.50 ☐
A TASTE OF LIFE	Julie Stafford	£3.50 ☐

All Sphere books are available at your local bookshop or newsagent, or can be ordered direct from the publisher. Just tick the titles you want and fill in the form below.

Name_____

Address_____

_____

Write to Sphere Books, Cash Sales Department, P.O. Box 11, Falmouth, Cornwall TR10 9EN

Please enclose a cheque or postal order to the value of the cover price plus:

UK: 60p for the first book, 25p for the second book and 15p for each additional book ordered to a maximum charge of £1.90.

OVERSEAS & EIRE: £1.25 for the first book, 75p for the second book and 28p for each subsequent title ordered.

BFPO: 60p for the first book, 25p for the second book plus 15p per copy for the next 7 books, thereafter 9p per book.

Sphere Books reserve the right to show new retail prices on covers which may differ from those previously advertised in the text elsewhere, and to increase postal rates in accordance with the P.O.